Healing Their Amish Hearts

Leigh Bale

P9-DIY-658

LOVE INSPIRED

INSPIRATIONAL ROMANCE

ISBN-13: 978-1-335-48800-8

Healing Their Amish Hearts

Copyright © 2020 by Lora Lee Bale

This edition published by arrangement with Harlequin Books S.A.

For questions and comments about the quality of this book, please contact us at CustomerService@Harlequin.com.

Love Inspired
22 Adelaide St. West, 40th Floor
Toronto, Ontario M5H 4E3, Canada
www.Harlequin.com

Printed in U.S.A.

"Sam, I have something special for you."

Becca rummaged inside one of her burlap bags before pulling out the pile of books the little boy had abandoned at the library.

Sam made a happy sound in the back of his throat and took the books onto his lap.

"And this is for you." She pulled out the book Jesse had been perusing and held it up for his inspection.

Jesse went very still. He wasn't sure if he should be happy or sad. He'd wanted to check out the book but he didn't want it forced down his throat by the pretty schoolteacher.

"I know you were in a big hurry to get home, so I thought I could check them out for you," she said.

She smiled and spoke so happily that Jesse didn't have the heart to scold her for being presumptuous. Her gesture was kind and he realized she only had their best interests at heart.

He spoke low, forcing himself to say the word *"Danke."*

"You're *willkomm.*"

No matter how hard he tried not to, Jesse liked her.

Leigh Bale is a *Publishers Weekly* bestselling author. She is the winner of the prestigious Golden Heart® Award and was a finalist for the Gayle Wilson Award of Excellence and the Booksellers' Best Award. The daughter of a retired US forest ranger, she holds a BA in history. Married in 1981 to the love of her life, Leigh and her professor husband have two children and two grandkids. You can reach her at leighbale.com.

Visit the Author Profile page at Harlequin.com for more titles.

Lo, children are an heritage of the Lord.
—*Psalm* 127:3

This book is dedicated to all those faithful couples who love, adore and cherish one another with a loyalty that surpasses anything this life or the dark forces can throw at them. They cling to one another and put the other first, second only to God, and love one another as the Savior taught us to do.

Chapter One

Starting a new job was never easy. But for Rebecca Graber, it seemed her first week as the interim teacher of the Amish school in Riverton, Colorado, might also be her last.

Standing beside her desk in the one-room schoolhouse, she picked up her McGuffey reader. Thirty old-fashioned wooden desks sat lined up in orderly fashion with a black potbellied stove at the front of the room. A wide chalkboard covered the front wall, topped with English and German penmanship charts and several pull-down maps and illustrations for lessons. Poetry, artwork and Amish proverbs dotted the other walls. Becca had plenty of paper, crayons and flash cards for the children to use. And sitting on her desk was a large handbell she rang when she called the children in from recess.

"First and second grades, please take out your reading books. All other grades will study quietly in their workbooks," she said.

There was a slight rustling as the twenty-four

scholars did as she asked. She didn't have a lot of students but since this was her first week teaching here, it felt closer to forty. On Monday morning, her first day here, her lesson plans had mysteriously disappeared. On Tuesday, she'd sat on a tack that had appeared on her chair. And the day after that, she had to break up a fight during recess when Caleb and Enos were teasing Sam. Yesterday, she'd found a paper taped to the back of her sweater that said *kick me*. No wonder the children had snickered every time she'd turned away. If she couldn't get control of her class soon, she had no doubt the school board would dismiss her as a complete and utter failure even before the first of May when school let out for the summer.

The room was tidy, with dark tan walls and wooden floors. The red log building had been a specially ordered kit that was built by the fathers of the scholars. Bike racks and a hitching post were situated out front in the graveled parking lot. A small barn stood near the outhouse where the children's horses and ponies were kept until it was time to go home. A spacious dirt area served as a baseball field. Although the school possibly needed a couple of swings and teeter-totter, Becca couldn't ask for more and wished this was a permanent position. But the regular teacher would return next fall, after she healed from the buggy accident that had crushed her pelvis and broken both her legs. The young woman was blessed to still be alive.

As she waited for the students to settle themselves, Becca glanced out the wide windows. The afternoon sun sparkled against the dusting of snow they'd received early that morning. The azure sky looked crystal clear but the February temperatures were downright frigid. Becca added another piece of wood to the fire, then called on a student to begin.

"Samuel King, would you please read out loud for us?" she asked with a kind smile.

Sam's soft brown eyes widened in panic, then he looked down at his book, his hands folded tightly in his lap. Becca waited patiently but the six-year-old boy didn't speak. Not a single word.

"Excuse me, Teacher Becca." Andy Yoder, the bishop's youngest son and another first-grader, held up his hand.

"Yes, Andy?" Becca asked.

"Sam don't talk, teacher. Not ever," Andy said.

"Sam *doesn't* talk," she said, correcting the boy's grammar.

And she wasn't willing to accept that. But first things first. She reached for a piece of chalk so she could write the correct sentence on the board. Finding no chalk, she pulled open the drawer to her desk…and quickly jerked back as a shrill cry escaped her throat.

A snake! In her desk drawer.

She stepped back so fast that her chair toppled to the floor. All the scholars gaped at her in surprise. A few snickered. Becca blinked, expecting the snake to move. But it didn't. And after closer inspection, she realized it was made of rubber.

A toy snake! In her desk drawer.

With a quick twist of her hand, she flipped it

out onto the floor. It landed near Caleb Yoder, the bishop's eleven-year-old son. He scooped it up before shoving it into one of the girls' faces. Absolute pandemonium erupted. The girl reared back and screamed as Caleb tossed the fake reptile to Enos Albrecht, who laughed and waved it in the air.

"Enos! Stop that," Becca called in a stern voice, trying to restore order.

Screeching madly, little Fannie Albrecht jumped up on her chair, her fisted hands pulled to her face in absolute terror. Shrieks and shouts filled the air.

"Stop that!" Reuben Fisher cried.

Reuben was the son of Becca's cousin and lived in the same house with her and her aunt Naomi. He tried to snatch the toy away from Enos but wasn't tall enough. In the struggle, the fake serpent bounced against the boy's hand and landed on the wooden floor in front of the door.

There was a loud gasp and the room went absolutely still.

Jesse King, Sam's father, stood in front of the open door, holding his black felt hat in his hands. His gaze swept the room, his shrewd eyes showing that he understood exactly what had transpired. A corner of his mouth twitched and Becca thought he might laugh. But no. He looked too stern to find any humor in the moment. A chilly gust of wind accompanied his entrance and he pushed the portal closed with the point of his black work boot. Becca stared, thinking she imagined the man. When had he come inside? Probably during the chaos.

Oh, no! Why did he have to show up now? What must he think of her?

A moment of confusion fogged Becca's mind. She couldn't move. Couldn't breathe. She watched as if in slow motion as Mr. King leaned down and picked up the rubber snake. It dangled from his large hand and Becca couldn't contain a shiver of revulsion.

"Is this yours?" Looking directly at Becca, Mr. King spoke in *Deitsch*, the German dialect their Amish people used among themselves. His voice sounded low and calm and he seemed completely unruffled by the horrible snake.

Mortified beyond words, Becca hurried toward him. Her face heated up like road flares. The fact that one of the fathers of her scholars had witnessed this shameful moment almost undid her.

"No, but I'll take care of it." She spoke in perfect English, the language they used in the classroom.

She forced herself to take the toy snake between two trembling fingers. With disgust, she returned it to the front of the room and shut it up in her desk drawer again. Out of her peripheral vision, she saw Lenore Schwartz help little Fannie climb down off her chair and the children all took their seats. And just like that, order was restored.

Gathering her composure, Becca patted her white organdy prayer *kapp* and smoothed her lavender skirts before she faced Sam's father again.

"Mr. King, was there something you wanted?" She lifted her chin higher, forcing herself to meet Jesse King's solid gaze. For just a moment, she thought his eyes looked sad and…haunted.

This was the first time she'd met him, though she'd seen him from afar on several occasions. Since she'd only arrived in Riverton eight days earlier, she hadn't had the opportunity to attend church yet but she'd tried to speak with him yesterday when he'd picked up Sam from school. He'd driven away before she could catch him and, if she didn't know better, she'd think he'd been trying to avoid her.

Up close, she realized he was a tall man with dark brooding eyes, high cheekbones and a narrow chin. His black hair was overly long for an Amish man and curled against the sides of his face. His beard indicated he was married, though Becca had been told by a member of the school board that he was a widower. Becca figured there was no one at home to cut his hair for him. If only he would smile, she might find him ruggedly handsome. But just now, his angular face showed no emotion whatsoever and only his eyes indicated an active mind hidden beneath his tranquil exterior.

"I've come to pick up Sam," Jesse said. His voice sounded low, his dark eyes unwavering.

Like her, Jesse and Sam were newcomers to this *Gmay*, their Amish community. They had moved here from Lancaster County in Pennsylvania just two months earlier. Apparently Jesse had lost his wife and two young daughters in a house fire a year earlier. The poor man. No wonder he looked so sad. And since that time, little Samuel hadn't spoken a single word. Becca knew no more than that. But she kept giving Sam opportunities and hoping that one day he would surprise her and finally read out loud.

Trying to be professional, she glanced at the clock on the wall. "But school isn't out for another twenty minutes. If you'd like to wait, perhaps I can speak with you afterward."

Jesse inclined his head. "*Ne*, I'm afraid I don't have time to wait. This afternoon, I need to move a boulder from my south field and won't be finished before it's time to return and pick him up from school. I'll have to take him home now."

Becca blinked. She was trying to be understanding. Trying to be a good teacher. But the truth was, she was highly inexperienced. Though she'd served four months as a teacher's apprentice in Ohio, this was her first time teaching solo. It was bad enough to come into a classroom full of scholars she didn't know but she had also entered this class midway through the school year. She wanted to do a good job. She really did. In fact, her future depended on it.

"Of course." She glanced at Sam, stepping over to help the boy gather his lunch pail and put on his warm winter coat.

For just a moment, Becca wished she was anywhere but here. She should be married and looking forward to raising a *familye* of her own, but that wasn't possible now. Not since her ex-fiancé had broken off their engagement. She'd known and loved Vernon all her life, yet he'd chosen to wed another girl they'd grown up with. If Becca failed in this position, she'd be forced to return to her *familye* in Ohio in shame. She was hoping for a good job reference so she could go elsewhere. She couldn't bear to go home and watch Vernon and Ruth marry and raise a *familye* together while she became a dried-up old spinster.

As she accompanied Sam to the door, she walked with him outside onto the front steps. "Mr. King, I really need to speak with you about Sam. Did you receive the letter I sent home with him two days ago?"

Jesse nodded. "*Ja*, I received your letter."

"*Gut.* Then you know I'd like to discuss Sam's problem…"

"Not now." Without another word, Jesse placed his hat on his head and hurried down the steps. Sam trailed behind.

Becca shivered and wrapped her arms around herself. Something hardened inside of her. She was Sam's teacher and must look after his education. Determined not to be ignored, she followed Jesse.

"If not now, when? I'm concerned about Sam. He's not speaking. I'd like to help," she called to Jesse's back.

Without a backward glance, the man climbed into his black buggy and closed the door. Sam scrambled into the buggy on the opposite side with a little difficulty. Becca helped him in, thinking it a bit derelict for a parent to let their six-year-old son fend for himself. She rounded the buggy, intending to confront the boy's father.

"Mr. King, please," she said.

Jesse took the leather lead lines into his large hands. Becca noticed several ugly, purple scars on his skin before he gave a little flick and the buggy lurched into motion. She had no choice but to step back or be trampled as he directed the horse down the muddy road. Within moments, they disappeared from view.

Well, of all the nerve! What a rude man.

Trying to hide her frustration, Becca turned and went inside. She was surprised to find the classroom so quiet. Every student had their head ducked over their books, the younger children studying their McGuffey readers while the older children wrote out vocabulary words.

No doubt the culprits of the snake incident must fear her wrath. She thought Caleb Yoder must be the ringleader. But without proof, she couldn't accuse him openly. Still, after the events of the past week, this wasn't the first time. And now there was a toy snake in her desk drawer. What would the school board say about that?

Being more cautious, she glanced at her chair before sitting down, then breathed a silent sigh of relief. Only ten more minutes and she'd be free for the weekend. Most of the children were bright, helpful and quiet. But Caleb and Enos had a penchant for causing enough trouble that Becca was seriously considering speaking with their parents. The only problem was that Caleb's father was Bishop Yoder. And she hated the thought of approaching the bishop of her new *Gmay* about his wayward son. No, she must handle this on her own. She had to get control of the school. And fast.

Standing again, she was determined to say something to the students. After all, it was her job to correct poor behavior. Choosing her words carefully, she folded her hands in front of her starched white apron.

"Scholars, I must tell you that I'm ashamed of you today. When Mr. King came to our school, we showed him what poorly behaved children you are. You embarrassed yourselves and I have no doubt your parents will hear all about it."

There. That was good. Maybe the fear of their parents finding out might make the children behave better. From the front of the room, Caleb slid lower in his seat. Perhaps the thought of his father hearing what had happened didn't appeal to him. Good! Maybe he'd think twice before putting tacks on her chair or rubber snakes in her drawer again.

"I hope as you go home this afternoon, you'll think about what your parents expect from you," she continued. "And I hope you won't let this happen again. Now, it's time to go home. Please tidy your desks and get your coats on. School is dismissed."

The students did as asked, hurrying toward the door. Out of her peripheral vision, Becca saw Caleb's elder brother nudge his arm, a look of disapproval on his face. Karen, who was Caleb's older sister, frowned as well.

Great! Becca wanted to cry out in victory. If Becca's admonitions wouldn't work, perhaps sibling pressure might help correct Caleb's poor behavior.

The last student headed out the door. Through the wide windows, Becca saw several black buggies waiting. Since the school was situated in one corner of Bishop Yoder's hay field, his farm was nearby. But this certainly wasn't like her home in Ohio where everyone lived within walking distance of the school. Many of the children here in Riverton lived as many as nine miles away and needed a ride home. Some children brought a small pony cart to school, while others waited for their parents to pick them up with their horse and buggy.

Returning to her desk, Becca stared at the place where she'd stowed the toy snake. With a quick jerk, she pulled the drawer open and recoiled in anticipation. But there was no need. During the brief time when she'd been outside speaking with Jesse King, the snake had disappeared.

Hmm. No doubt one of the children had taken it. And honestly, Becca was happy to have it gone. Hopefully it didn't make a reappearance. Because she desperately wanted the school board to write her a nice reference when she finished her assignment in May. She needed to serve as a substitute teacher for three full years before being eligible to teach at any Amish parochial school. As a teacher, she was a late bloomer. She hadn't done any student teaching earlier, when she'd first achieved her certificate of completion from the Amish school she'd attended as a girl. She thought she'd be getting married, so she hadn't even considered it at the time. But if she did well here in Riverton, she could get an Amish teaching job anywhere. This position was only a beginning, but she'd do almost anything to keep from returning home to Ohio.

Now, if she could just figure out a way to handle Jesse King and little Sam's lack of speech, she might have a chance.

Jesse patted the side of his black-and-white Holstein and picked up the two buckets of fresh milk. Carrying them outside the barn, he noticed the skiff of snow they'd had that morning had almost melted off. It'd be dark soon. The afternoon sun was settling behind the Wet Mountains to the east. The fading beams of light sprayed the sky in creamy pink and gold, glinting off the jagged spikes of granitic rock. Jesse had been reading up on his new home. The Wet Valley sat at an elevation of just under 8,000 feet. With the cooler elevation and much shorter growing season, he'd never be able to successfully grow anything but hay, some barley and maybe some sugar beets. In his summer garden, the snap peas and carrots should do fine, but some other Amish farmers at church had told him not to bother growing celery and he'd have to cover his tomato plants at night or they'd freeze. But his farmland was fertile and located ten long miles outside of town. Because his new home was isolated and lonely, he'd gotten it for a cheap price. And the solitude was just what he wanted to soothe his broken heart.

Still holding the milk buckets, he paused, remembering the last time he'd shared a similar sunset with his sweet wife, Alice. Back then, they'd been living in the overly populated area of Lancaster County. They'd been walking from the barn to their house when he'd pulled her close as they'd admired the beauty of *Gott's* creations. They'd heard about this new Amish settlement in Colorado and talked about moving here. It'd provide more opportunities for growth. A place where they could expand and their *familye* would have a better future. They were happy and filled with anticipation. Life was so good then.

Alice and their two daughters had died three days later, taking all of Jesse's joy with them.

The rattle of a horse and buggy drew his attention. He turned and groaned out loud. Rebecca Graber, Sam's schoolteacher, was just pulling into his graveled driveway.

He thought about rushing inside and pretending he didn't know she was here. He could ignore her knock on the door. But no. He'd have to face her sooner or later.

Setting the buckets of frothy milk on the back porch, he tucked his thumbs into the black suspenders that crossed his blue chambray shirt and waited. Becca pulled up right in front of him and climbed out of her buggy. Wearing a heavy black mantle with a gray scarf wrapped around her neck, she tugged off her gloves. Taking a step, she tucked several golden-blond strands of hair back into her black traveling bonnet. Other than her bright pink cheeks and nose, her skin looked smooth and pale as porcelain. Her startling blue eyes sparkled with a zest for life, her heart-shaped lips creased in a tentative smile.

"*Hallo*, Mr. King," she called.

"*Hallo*. What can I do for you?" he returned with little enthusiasm.

Slightly breathless, she joined him next to the back door. "I was hoping to speak with you briefly about Sam. I'm guessing you've noticed he doesn't speak. I'd like to help. And I think if we team up, we can be more effective."

Something hardened inside of Jesse. Who did this woman think she was? Coming to his home to tell him how to raise his son.

"How old are you?" he asked.

She blinked at his odd question. "I'm twenty-two.

But I don't see what that has to do with Sam's reluctance to speak."

Hmm. She was just four years younger than Jesse. Since age eighteen was the norm for schoolteachers, he thought her quite old. And he couldn't help wondering why she wasn't already married. A pretty little thing like her should have no trouble finding a willing groom. Especially here in Colorado, where Amish women were scarce. But he told himself he didn't care. It wasn't his business and he had bigger problems on his mind right now.

"I'm a fairly new teacher but I do know my subjects quite well. I just want to help," Becca said.

"I doubt anything can be done for Sam," he said, trying to keep his voice even and calm. "He'll speak again once he's *gut* and ready."

Becca shook her head. "I don't think so, Mr. King. When did Sam stop speaking?"

A rush of sad memories flooded his mind and he looked away. Her question seemed too personal. The pain was still so raw that it felt like it had happened just yesterday. "It started the afternoon of his mother and sisters' funeral."

She made a sad little crooning sound, like the coo of a dove. "*Ach*, I'm so very sorry. I have no doubt that was traumatic and difficult for both of you."

She didn't know the half of it. Sam had started the fire. It was his fault his mother and sisters had died. His fault they were now alone in this cold, ramshackle house. But Becca's compassion was more than Jesse could stand. Over the past year, so many people had expressed their condolences. Then they'd

introduced him to another eligible woman, as if anyone could take Alice's place in his life. And that was
just the problem. He didn't want another wife. He
didn't want to ever marry again. He just wanted to
be left alone. That was the whole reason he'd relocated to Colorado in the first place.

"I really don't think there's anything you can do
for Sam. It'd be best if you just leave him alone and
he'll start to speak again when he's ready." Jesse
turned to go inside but she stopped him, placing a
gentle hand on his arm for just a moment.

"I don't think so, Mr. King. I'm sure there are
things we can do to help," she said.

"*Ne*, I've already had two doctors take a look at
him and there's no physical reason he can't speak.
He's just decided to stop talking," Jesse insisted.

"It's *gut* that you've had him visit some doctors
but there's obviously something wrong. Though I've
never dealt with a traumatic problem, I worked with
a couple of special needs children in Ohio and I believe Sam needs some extra help."

So. She wasn't going to let this go. Though Jesse
was a new member of the *Gmay* here in Riverton and
had attended Sunday church meetings, he'd stayed
apart and hadn't yet developed any real friendships
with the other Amish families. Instead, he'd buried
his heartache in hard work. Easy to do, considering the dilapidated condition of his new farm. Since
he'd moved here two months earlier, he'd spent every
waking moment mending the house, barn and broken fences. He still needed to repair the leaky roof
and build furniture for his cold, ramshackle home.

Having lost most of his possessions in the house fire, he'd had to start from scratch. And amidst all of that, he'd had to look after Sam, driving the boy back and forth to school, preparing meals, washing laundry and a myriad of other chores his wife used to do. There'd been a lot to deal with on his own.

Thankfully, he'd been able to sell his smaller farm in Pennsylvania to a neighbor, which had allowed him to purchase this new, bigger place in Colorado. And right now, he needed to get back to work.

The screen door on the back of the house clapped closed as Sam came outside. Jesse barely glanced at the boy, trying to think of something to say that would make Becca Graber go away and leave him alone. Instead, she smiled at Sam, so brightly that Jesse could only stare at her for several seconds. Bending at the waist, she looked the boy in the eyes.

"*Hallo*, Sam. How are you?" she asked.

The boy's eyes widened, his face creased with worry. He shuffled his feet, looking anxious. A few gurgling sounds came from the back of his throat but he couldn't seem to get any words out. Finally, he jabbed a finger urgently at the house and Becca gasped.

"*Gucke!* Something is burning," she cried.

Jesse turned and saw billows of black smoke rushing from the open doorway of the kitchen. Oh, no! The pork chops. They must be burning. He'd completely forgotten all about them.

"Stay here," he commanded as he raced into the house.

A thick fog of black smoke emanated from the metal frying pan sitting on top of the gas stove and filled the kitchen. As a certified firefighter, Jesse knew what to do. He reached into the cupboard beneath the sink and pulled out a Class B kitchen fire extinguisher. Aiming the nozzle, he blasted the burning pan with a fog of fire retardant. Then, he picked up the metal lid and, angling it to protect his face, slid it over the top of the pan to snuff out the grease fire. Lastly, he switched off the burner and slid the pan away from the source of heat.

A light tapping came from the open doorway and Becca poked her head in. "Is it safe to come in now?"

She stood there holding Sam's hand, waiting for Jesse's permission to enter. He nodded, wishing she'd go away. This had been a simple grease fire but it had brought the past right back for him. The night Alice and their two daughters had been killed, he was off fighting a house fire somewhere else. If only he'd been home that night, he might have saved them. It was his fault they were gone. It had been his job to protect them. His job to keep them safe.

And he'd failed.

His body trembled as he stood looking at the charred remnants of the four pork chops. He'd put the meat on the lowest heat, thinking they'd be fine until he returned from the barn. Now, he had nothing to feed Sam for supper.

He glanced at Becca and saw her gazing at his hands. Reddish-purple scars covered his skin, extending up both of his forearms. A cruel reminder that he'd run into a burning house to try and save his wife and daughters.

He folded his arms, hiding the ugly scars. Without speaking, Becca quietly opened all the windows and doors, allowing the chilly breeze to clear the house of smoke. As if from a distance, Jesse watched her silently. No matter how hard he clenched them, he couldn't stop his hands from shaking.

Becca directed little Sam to put on his coat until the room could be warmed up again. With rapt attention, the boy followed her every move as she built up the fire in the potbellied stove.

She glanced at Jesse and hesitated. From her sympathetic expression, he was certain she could see the truth inside him. That he was upset. Shaken by the grease fire. He felt suddenly exposed. The moment was too personal. Too private. Because it hit too close to home. A reminder of what had happened a year earlier when he'd lost everyone in his *familye*, except Sam. And he didn't want Becca Graber to see that. Or to know what he tried so hard to hide.

"You should leave," he said, feeling grouchy.

"You'll need something else for supper." She spoke in that soft, efficient voice of hers.

Without permission, she stepped over to the cupboards and opened the doors, peering inside. He knew she would find them as empty as his broken heart. She opened the fridge before lifting her eyebrows in a dubious expression.

"Is this all the food you have in the house?" she asked, gesturing to the skimpy remnants of a ham and a small chunk of Swiss cheese.

"That and the milk." Jesse retrieved the two buckets and set them on the counter by the sink. Having a chore to do helped soothe his jangled nerves.

Alice had always made their butter and cheese.

Jesse knew the process but didn't have time to sit and churn milk into curd. And the few times he had done so, it didn't taste right when he finished. Something was missing.

Alice, Mary and Susanna were gone.

Pulling the ham and cheese from the fridge, Becca set them on the counter. She paused for just a moment, looking at the sink filled with dirty dishes. Without recriminations, she picked up a horse harness he had been mending and carried it to set beside the back door. Then, she rolled up her sleeves and quickly washed two plates and glasses.

"I noticed you have a coop but it doesn't look like you have any chickens on your place, so you don't have any eggs." She spoke as she worked. "Maybe in the spring you can get some baby chicks. But this will do for tonight."

Yes, he planned to buy some chickens next week. He also wanted to buy pigs, draft horses and another milk cow once the weather warmed up. But for now, he'd have to make do. A trip to the grocery store in town was definitely on the agenda for the morning. He'd stock up so this didn't happen again.

Becca shivered and Jesse placed another stick of wood in the potbellied stove. His home wasn't much to look at. The walls were dingy and scarred, the rooms devoid of furniture. Upstairs in the bedrooms, he'd laid two mattresses on the bare wood floors for him and Sam to sleep. No chairs. No chests of drawers. No armoires, curtains, rugs or wall hangings. The house had been uninhabited for six years. He'd been told the previous owner was *Englisch* and couldn't make a go of the place. But Jesse was willing to work hard and didn't need much to earn a simple living for him and Sam. He'd bought the farm cheap from a foreclosure sale and was glad to have it.

Becca set out the last six slices of his store-bought bread and layered them with wedges of ham and cheese for sandwiches. It'd be a dry meal but they could wash the food down with plenty of milk.

Watching her slender hands work, he thought about how much he missed Alice's homemade breads, biscuits, pies and cakes.

"Here you go." Becca set the two plates on the table and directed Sam to sit.

The boy gave her a questioning glance, his eyes wide, his little face so sweet and innocent. Jesse dearly loved his son. He truly did. But Sam was a constant reminder of all that they'd lost. Because Sam had set the fire. And though Jesse knew it wasn't right, he couldn't help blame the boy. He'd tried to forgive his son just as he'd tried to forgive himself. He really had. But he hadn't been able to do so. Not yet, anyway.

"Ahem, will you join us?" Jesse asked, trying to be polite but wishing she'd go now.

"*Ne*, I'll eat when I get home. This is for you," Becca said.

Surprised by how she seemed to have taken over his home, Jesse joined Sam at the table. Within a few moments, they had bowed their heads and blessed the food. Jesse didn't know what else to do. While Becca poured his son a glass of milk right from the pail, Sam immediately picked up his ham sandwich and took a big bite.

"I'm going to head home now." Becca spoke to Jesse. "It's getting dark outside and the roads will turn icy. I think you and I should speak more in depth at another time when you aren't so…indisposed."

Jesse nodded eagerly. "*Ja*, another time, perhaps."

But she didn't move. Didn't take a single step toward the door. Instead, she closed the windows above the sink, seeming satisfied that enough smoke had dissipated from the house. Since it was wintertime, the days were shorter and it was already getting dark outside. She lit two kerosene lamps. The wicks flickered, sending eerie shadows to chase around the room. He could see her curious gaze as she peered into every corner. A feeling of mortification washed over him. He was highly conscious of the run-down condition of his home. And more than ever, he missed Alice's home bottled beans, corn, peaches and tomatoes. She'd cared for their children and kept their home running with methodical order. But like everything else, it had all gone up in smoke.

"I… I've been kinda busy. I haven't had time to go into town to the grocery store. And I haven't had time yet to repair and paint some of the holes in the walls." He sat there, his thumbs looped through his suspenders.

She brushed past him. He caught her scent…a clean, citrusy smell that he kind of liked. "I understand completely. It must be difficult being on your own in a new place with a little boy to raise. But don't worry. You'll get things in order soon." She spoke in a cheerful, positive voice as she picked up the pair of gloves she'd set aside earlier when she'd prepared their supper.

Finally. Finally she stepped toward the outside door. Jesse stood and followed, breathing a silent sigh of relief. She was really leaving this time. But she stopped at the door and turned, catching him unaware. As he gazed down into her beautiful blue eyes, he couldn't help comparing her to Alice. The two women were so different. Alice had been filled with inner strength but she'd been shy, quiet and unassuming. So different from Becca, who was rather bossy, outgoing and quick to take matters into her own hands.

"Mr. King, until we can make a more formal plan of action, I'd like to suggest that you read to Sam each evening. Try to get him to read to you as well. I really think that would help for the time being," she said.

Read to Sam? Jesse didn't have time for such nonsense but didn't say so. He wasn't interested in taking advice from an inexperienced schoolteacher like Becca Graber, no matter how attractive she was. But he nodded.

He accompanied her outside but didn't help as she climbed into her buggy. He didn't think it would be appropriate to touch her. With a wave of her hand, she bid him farewell and her horse took off at a jaunty trot.

Jesse stood there, watching her go. And as she turned onto the main county road, he breathed a deep sigh of relief. He couldn't help feeling as if a tornado had just swept through his home. Rebecca Graber. What a dynamo. Jesse chuckled, thinking that another fire wouldn't dare invade his new house. Because if it did, Tornado Becca would just sweep it away.

Chapter Two

Becca pulled another dusty book off the shelf and promptly sneezed. Flipping through the front table of contents, she read each topic, searching for anything that might help Sam King. After a few moments, she added this text to her growing pile. She had chosen at least six good books on vocabulary and selective mutism and how to help children who wouldn't speak.

Standing inside the town library, she perused a bulleted list on a tip sheet, her mind churning. The little bit she'd learned that morning was not what she'd expected. Not at all. Selective mutism wasn't a problem where a child refused to speak in order to get attention. Nor was the child acting naughty. Rather, such children had an anxiety disorder wherein they couldn't speak because their apprehension was so severe they were actually scared silent.

Flipping to a chapter on treatment, she braced the book against the shelf and continued reading. It was Saturday morning and she'd taken advantage of the clear weather to come into town and see what she might find. She could check out library books, as long as they magnified Jesus Christ. Jakob Fisher, her first cousin, had driven her here but she'd have to walk back to his farm. She lived with Jakob, his wife and three children, her aunt and grandfather. If she found some help for Sam today, the nine-mile walk home would be worth it.

An hour earlier, she'd paid a quick visit to Caroline Schwartz, Sam's permanent teacher. The poor girl was still in the hospital, her legs and hips in traction. If Caroline hoped to walk again, she'd be restricted to bed for the next four months. At barely eighteen years of age, Caroline seemed even more inexperienced at teaching than Becca. And since the accident had happened about the same time Jesse and Sam had moved to the area, Caroline hadn't yet been able to do anything about the boy's problem. She'd explained to Becca that she'd ordered a newsletter written by Amish parents of special needs children titled *Life's Special Sunbeams*. That might be of some help but Becca doubted it. Still, she had the address of the national publication and planned to subscribe as well.

Caroline had also tried to speak with Jesse King but the man had terrified her with his offish manner. No surprise there. Jesse didn't seem to like anyone. But Becca wasn't about to let the oafish man scare her off. She was determined to do something to help Sam, with or without his father's cooperation. She believed Sam's unwillingness to speak had everything to do with his mother and sisters' deaths.

Lifting the pile of books, Becca carried them back to the open area of the library. Her mind buzzed with a number of techniques she'd like to try with Sam. Ritual greetings every morning at school, including him in activities even if he didn't speak and some other techniques to reduce his anxiety while at school. She had some flash cards she could use but thought she might need to spend extra time working one-on-one with Sam when the other children weren't around to distract or startle him. And she wasn't sure how to build that time into the school curriculum. It wouldn't be prudent to ignore the other children's needs because Sam required so much extra attention but she'd figure it out.

Making her way back to the table where she'd been jotting down notes, she thought of a possible solution…and promptly bumped into someone.

"Oof!"

She looked up and blinked. "Mr. King."

He stared down at her with widened eyes, seeming just as surprised as she was. "*Hallo*, Miss Graber."

"Wh…what are you doing here?" she asked, thinking how nonsensical she sounded.

He shifted his weight and she saw that he held a book in his hand. He quickly lowered his arm, shielding the text behind his thigh. From his nervous gesture, she thought he was trying to conceal it from her. But he didn't know her very well. Reaching behind him, she took the book from his hand and read the title out loud.

"The Silent Child."

His face flushed red as a sugar beet. Ah, he wasn't as withdrawn from his son's problem as he made it appear. In fact, it looked as though he was actually trying to do something to help Sam. And right then and there, Becca's opinion of Jesse King improved just a tad. Up to now, she'd had little respect for the man but realized he wasn't the uncaring, brutish father he appeared to be. But why did he have to be so difficult about it? Why did he have to hide his concern? It seemed as though he were fighting against himself. As though he didn't want to care about Sam, yet he did. Very much.

She met his gaze, noticing the irritated glint in his eyes. She could tell that he didn't like meeting her here. She held the book out to him and he took it reluctantly.

"It looks like you're reading up on Sam's problem." She spoke the obvious.

"*Ja*, I thought maybe..." He didn't finish the sentence. "What are you doing here?" he asked instead.

She held up several books on the same topic. "The same as you. Looking for ways to help Sam."

He snorted. "I doubt it'll do any *gut*. I've already tried everything I can think of and Sam still won't talk. He hasn't said a single word in almost a year."

"I'm sorry."

He shrugged and looked away but not before she saw the pain written in his eyes. Her heart gave a painful squeeze. The poor little boy. And the poor man too! This couldn't be easy on Jesse either.

"But we have to try, don't we?" she asked.

He glanced at his son, who sat a short distance

away at another table, poring over several children's books. The boy's lips were moving and Becca got the impression he was reading to himself. She'd seen him do this in school before but what it meant, she had no idea.

"It appears that he can read," she observed.

"*Ja*, his *mudder* taught him. She…she used to read to all our *kinder* all the time. Sam can definitely read."

Hmm. Was that why Jesse seemed so against reading to Sam each night? Because it was something his wife had done before she died? Or was it simply because he was busy and thought reading to his son was a woman's job? Well, it was time to teach him differently. Fathers could read to their kids just as well as mothers.

"Are you planning to read to Sam each night, as we discussed?" she asked.

"I… I don't have a lot of extra time. By the time I finish my barn chores, Sam's usually half-asleep. And I've been trying to make us some furniture in the evenings," he hedged.

Becca didn't argue. She sensed that she couldn't push Jesse King any more than she could little Sam. But still, Jesse had come to the library to check out some books. That was a good start.

"Any idea how well Sam can read?" Becca asked.

He shrugged those unbelievably wide shoulders of his. "*Ne*, I have no idea. I just know he can read. He was always a bright little fellow before…"

Before his momma died. That was good. If they could just get Sam to speak again, it could open up a whole new world for the boy. And possibly open the world again to Jesse King too.

He sidestepped her, edging toward his son. "Um, we were just leaving. We have to get home soon."

"But I was hoping to meet with you at length. Is there a time when you and I can sit down and develop a plan of action for Sam?"

He shook his head. "Not today."

"But, Mr. King!" She took a step after him.

"Shh!" The librarian appeared out of nowhere, pressing a finger to her lips. From the stern lift of the woman's eyebrows, Becca realized she must have spoken too loudly.

Without another word, Jesse turned and hurried over to Sam. The man's black felt hat sat on the table top and he picked it up and placed it on his head. Becca watched in frustration, longing to go after him. Wanting to make him listen to her. But she knew she couldn't force him to do what he didn't want to do. And that's when something else occurred to her.

Sam didn't speak because he was traumatized by the deaths of his mother and sister. But Jesse King was just as traumatized in his own way. And he obviously didn't want to talk about it. She could empathize with the man. Losing his wife and daughters must have scarred his heart as much as it had Sam's. And that's when she decided to give Jesse some space. He'd been reluctant to help, yet he'd come to the library on his own. With a little more time, maybe he would seek out her assistance as well. But for Sam's sake, she hoped Jesse didn't wait too long.

"Come on, Sam." Jesse spoke low as he took the boy's arm and tugged gently.

Sam had no choice but to follow and he reluctantly left his books behind. As they headed toward the front door, he looked back at the texts with such longing that Becca knew he wasn't finished with them yet. She couldn't help wondering why Jesse seemed so antisocial. Every time she tried to talk to him, he acted skittish, like he wanted to get away. Or was it just her he didn't like? She wasn't sure but it seemed to her that Jesse fought against himself. Some inner strife seemed to wage a battle inside of him. She figured it all must relate to his deceased wife and daughters.

She watched as they hurried out of the library without a single book in tow. Even Jesse had abandoned the text he'd been holding. It was such a shame. Both the father and son could benefit greatly from those texts. Becca decided to do something about it. Stepping over to Sam's table, she scooped up most of the plethora of books the child had been reading and carried them over to the checkout counter with her own selections. She added Jesse's book to the pile. No matter how hard he tried, Jesse King was not getting rid of her.

Jesse flicked the leather lead lines at his horse's rump and settled into his seat. After leaving the library, he'd taken Sam over to the grocery store and stocked up on numerous cases of canned and boxed goods. Soup, chili, corn, string beans, peaches, pears and oatmeal. Now, even if he did burn their supper, he'd have something in the house to feed his son. It wasn't that he didn't have money to buy food but rather he had too many chores to carry alone. He needed his wife and daughters back. He needed Alice more than ever.

The buggy-wagon swayed gently as he turned the horse off Main Street and headed along the county road. The clop of the horse's hooves hitting the black asphalt soothed his jangled nerves. He didn't know why he'd gone to the library in town. Sam had been delighted. Though the boy didn't speak, Jesse could see his pleasure written across his face and in the little skip in his stride. It had been a lapse in judgment and Jesse had been mortified to be caught there by Becca Graber. Having been raised by a strong, domineering father, Jesse didn't like feeling out of control. And that's how Sam's problem made him feel. Out of control.

Sam sat silently beside him on the front seat. Jesse knew his son wasn't happy to leave his books behind. Maybe he should have checked them out for the boy. Even if he didn't read to Sam, there was no reason to keep the child from reading on his own. They both already lived such a lonely, isolated life. The books might open up the world to Sam. They might help him speak again.

Maybe on Monday, Jesse could make another quick trip into town and check out the books for Sam. Wouldn't the boy be excited when he came home from school and found a pile of texts waiting for him?

The thought made Jesse go very still. He'd been

so angry at Sam for so long now that it was a novelty for him to want to make the boy happy. But he did. In fact, Jesse longed to hear his son's laughter again. How he wished his son would speak.

At that moment, Sam lifted an arm and pointed. Jesse could just make out a lone figure, walking ahead of them on the side of the road. From her plain dress, black tights, heavy shawl and bonnet, he could tell she was Amish. She carried a heavy bag in each hand. Probably walking home after shopping in town. But then he saw a flash of purple skirts and knew exactly who she was.

Becca Graber.

His shoulders tensed and he thought of driving on by without acknowledging her. But that would be too rude, even for him.

As his buggy-wagon neared, she glanced over her shoulder and moved a safe distance off the road so she wouldn't be trampled. He instantly regretted making her move as he watched her sidestep the muddy ground.

When he pulled up beside her, she stopped and nodded, her hands too encumbered by the heavy bags to wave.

"*Hallo*! Fancy meeting you out here on the road," she said.

Her voice held a happy lilt and he wondered vaguely if anything ever got her down.

"*Ja*, fancy that. You look as though your arms are quite full. Can we offer you a ride home?" Though his voice held little enthusiasm, Jesse forced himself to say the words, knowing it was the right thing to do.

She hesitated, glancing at the long road ahead. "Are you sure it's no trouble?"

He'd heard that she lived with the Fishers, who were her relatives. *Dawdi* Zeke, the eldest member of the *Gmay* at ninety-six years, was her grandfather. They lived nine miles outside of town and Jesse would pass right by their farm on his way home. Ironically, the Fishers were his neighbors. A fact that made it much too easy for Becca to drive over to their place whenever she wanted. He just hoped she didn't make a habit of popping in during the supper hour.

"*Ne,* of course not. We pass by your place on our way home. Climb in." The moment he made the invitation, he regretted it. He didn't want to give Sam's schoolteacher a ride home. He wanted to be left alone.

"*Ach, danke* so much. I didn't realize how heavy these books would be when I was sitting in the library." She handed the bags to him and he set them on the floor of the back seat.

As she climbed up to sit with Sam in between them, Jesse saw her glance back at the wagon. It was filled with boxes and bags of groceries, shingles and other roofing supplies, as well as a large crate of live chickens. The hens had fluffed their feathers and huddled together for warmth as they clucked with impatience. He didn't get into town often and had made the best of this trip.

"I see you've been to the grocery store and got some hens too," she said as she settled herself.

"*Ja.*" He flicked the leads at the horse's rump and they lurched forward.

"That's *gut*. At least you'll have fresh eggs to eat if you burn the pork chops again." She laughed, the sound high and sweet. There was no guile in her voice but simply a gentle sense of humor.

Jesse would have smiled but he still couldn't decide if he liked this woman. She was definitely likeable, if he weren't still missing Alice so much.

"Sam, I have something special for you." She reached around and rummaged inside one of her burlap bags before pulling out the pile of books the boy had abandoned at the library.

Sam made a happy sound in the back of his throat and took the books onto his lap.

"And this is for you." She pulled out the book Jesse had been perusing and held it up for his inspection.

Jesse went very still. He wasn't sure if he should be happy or sad. He'd wanted to check out the book but he didn't want it forced down his throat by the pretty schoolteacher.

"I know you were in a big hurry to get home, so I thought I could check them out for you," she said.

Hmm. Interesting how she was making this easy for him, as if he'd been indisposed so she'd done him a favor.

"I had planned to bring them to you at church tomorrow. Now you can read this evening. But you'll only be able to keep them for two weeks before they're due back at the library," she warned.

She smiled and spoke so happily that Jesse didn't have the heart to scold her for being presumptuous.

Her gesture was kind and he realized she only had their best interests at heart.

"Danke." He spoke low, forcing himself to say the word.

"You're *willkomm.*"

Turning in her seat, she perused the clear but chilly day. The afternoon sun had done its best to melt off the snow but slushy spots on the road would soon ice up as evening came on and he was eager to get home. Driving a horse and buggy at night was not safe. Cars and trucks traveled way too fast and might come upon them without seeing their reflective lights. He'd heard that Caroline Schwartz, the regular schoolteacher, had been driving a buggy at night when she was hit from behind. The accident had nearly killed the poor girl and they'd had to put her horse down.

"Isn't it a nice day?" Becca asked, then gave an exaggerated shiver. "But brrr, it's so cold. Still, it could always be worse. At least it isn't snowing again."

Jesse agreed but didn't answer. He just listened as Becca talked on and on about inconsequential things. The weather. Their church meetings tomorrow. The end-of-year program she was planning for the school. The box social fund-raiser she'd been asked to coordinate so they could purchase playground equipment for the school. He glanced at her pretty profile, thinking once again that she was like a whirl of wind. And he wasn't sure he liked that.

"Did you walk into town this morning?" he asked.

"Ne, my cousin, Jakob, gave me a ride. He needed

to buy supplies too. But I wanted to stay longer and told him I'd walk home this afternoon. Since the weather was clear, he agreed." She gazed out at the damp countryside. "I think at that time, I underestimated how cold it is outside. I walked everywhere when I lived in Ohio but I'm still not used to the colder weather in Colorado. And everything is so spread out here. My cousin's farm is much too far from town to walk in the cold and I won't make that mistake again."

He agreed. If she had been his cousin, he would not have let her walk nine miles on such a cold winter's day. And though he would never admit such a thing, it kind of upset him that Jakob Fisher had been so derelict in her care. Since he'd lived here for a number of years already, the man should have known better.

"I'm sorry. I'm talking too much, aren't I?" she said suddenly.

Yes, but he didn't say so. He would never admit that he liked her incessant chatter. It had been so long since he'd listened to a woman talk about everything and nothing and it filled up the lonely void of the ride. With Sam not speaking, Jesse's life had become overly quiet and he realized he was hungry to talk to someone. Anyone! Even if that someone happened to be Sam's pushy schoolteacher.

Before he knew it, they had arrived at the turnoff to the Fishers' farm. Jesse wasn't about to make Becca walk the muddy road leading to the house and he turned the horse down the lane. The two-story log structure looked just the same as his, except that it was in pristine repair. So was the large, red barn. The tidy property was outlined by long barbed wire fences and fallow fields waiting for spring plowing. Black-and-white milk cows stood in a corral, chewing their cud. Several draft horses stood together near a cluster of barren trees. In the summertime, he had no doubt the place would be burgeoning with green life.

One day soon, Jesse hoped his own farm looked in this good a shape but he knew it would take time and lots of hard work for it to prosper. But he intended to do just that. Bishop Yoder had offered to coordinate a work frolic to help with some of the repairs but Jesse had politely refused. He'd come here for isolation and didn't want a lot of people around his place asking a lot of questions about Alice and their girls. For now, he wanted to be left alone.

"*Danke* for the ride. I'll see you tomorrow at church." Becca hopped out after he pulled the horse to a stop in front of the house.

She reached up as Jesse handed her the bags. Their fingers brushed together for just a moment and he felt the warmth of her soft skin against his. Sam waved, but Jesse didn't speak. He didn't want to see Becca Graber again. And yet, he did. Not because he was interested in her as a woman. But rather, she was so different from Alice. So filled with ideas, so talkative and bright, like a shiny new button. Becca Graber was a novelty to him. A glimpse of normalcy that he hadn't enjoyed in a long, lonely time. And no matter how hard he tried not to, he liked her.

Chapter Three

Jesse awoke slowly, pulled out of a deep sleep. Opening his eyes, he blinked into the darkness. It was way too early to get up for morning chores. Over the past year, he hadn't been sleeping well. Tonight was no exception. He'd gone to bed late after working on another chair to go with the kitchen table. After tossing and turning for what seemed like hours, he'd fallen into a dreamless sleep. So, what had awakened him?

He rolled over, pulling the warm quilt with him. He gazed through the shadows at the empty pillow next to him. How he missed Alice and her warm, gentle touch. Just knowing she was there, lying beside him, had brought him joy. But now, the house felt cold and empty. He must have forgotten to stoke the fire in the stove before he went to bed. But honestly, he'd become skittish about adding kindling at night for fear it might start another house fire. Although he'd lost his previous home because Sam was playing with matches, he'd become overly cautious when it came to fire.

There! The sound came again. A low cry from the outer hallway followed by muffled crying. Sam must be having another nightmare.

Throwing back the covers, Jesse sat up and placed his bare feet against the chilly floor. Alice wasn't here to make one of her large rag rugs to cover the bare, scarred wood. He'd resisted buying one, trying to conserve his funds until the priority expenses had been met, such as repairing the leaky roof and buying more livestock. His future livelihood depended on him making this farm prosper and he intended to do just that.

Standing, he reached for his discarded shirt and pulled it over top of his undershirt. Raking a hand through his disheveled hair, he walked out onto the landing at the top of the stairs. He paused beside the door to Sam's bedroom and listened. Another scream and then pitiful weeping came from the room and he raced inside. Sam lay upon the mattress, his arms and legs tangled in the bedding. His eyes were closed in sleep but he thrashed around, as if he were trying to escape some unknown predator.

Definitely another nightmare. The boy had been having such bad dreams ever since the fire, though their occurrence had diminished once they'd arrived in Riverton. Over time, Jesse had hoped the bad dreams would disappear entirely.

He pulled the covers away and rearranged them before lying on the mattress with his son. Blanketing them both against the frigid night air, he pulled Sam into his arms, aware that the boy had awakened and was silently weeping. His slim body trembled, his shoulders quaking. Holding the child against his chest, Jesse rubbed his back the way Alice used to do whenever one of their children was sick or upset about something.

"Shh, *Daed* is here now. You're safe. It's going to be all right," Jesse soothed, copying her words.

Alice had always known what to do, what to say. Her kind, quiet nature had brought him comfort whenever he was worried about something too. She was the most caring, prim and proper woman he'd ever known. So different from Becca Graber's outgoing nature. And yet, Becca seemed no less kind and giving. She just went about it in different ways.

Sam's back and shoulders trembled, his tears wetting Jesse's neck. The boy curled his tiny hands into the folds of Jesse's shirt, as if he were clinging to a lifeline. Jesse continued to reassure the boy, speaking sentiments of comfort.

How he wished he could believe what he said. That everything would be all right. That the painful ache lodged inside their hearts would somehow ease and go away. But it hadn't. Not one bit. Because Alice, Mary and Susanna were all gone. And Jesse couldn't bring them back. He thought that relocating his son to Colorado would diminish the tender memories they each suffered from. That somehow, they could forget. But it was still there, raw and painful. Haunting them every day.

Jesse had been taught all his life to accept *Gott's* will. That he should be accepting of where divine Providence had placed him. It wasn't right for him to question *Gott's* motives in anything. But he did.

He couldn't help asking why Alice and his little girls had to die. Why?

Now, Jesse had only his faith to rely on. The belief that *Gott* had taken his *familye* into His hands and would love and care for them until they could all be reunited once more.

"Gott verlosst die Seine nicht." Jesse spoke the phrase softly, trying to believe that God would never abandon them.

Sam didn't respond. Didn't move a muscle or say a single word. But Jesse knew he heard and understood. Now, if only they could both believe his words, they might have some hope of healing.

An hour later, Jesse still lay there in the dark, staring up at the ceiling, wondering if it had been a good choice for him to bring Sam to Colorado. It was what he and Alice had talked about. What they had planned for some time. Their home and *familye* in Pennsylvania was gone and he'd thought to give them a fresh start somewhere that didn't remind him and Sam of all they'd lost. But even here, in a house that Alice and his girls had never lived in, Jesse still saw them every day in his mind and in his heart. The memories haunted him. And he realized then that they were such a part of him and Sam that neither of them could ever forget. Jesse couldn't seem to let them go. He could run and hide but they'd still be with him. He longed to run away, but he couldn't run from himself. So, how could he overcome the pain and regret and live again? He must have faith! He knew that without a doubt. Yet, it was so hard to put his beliefs into action.

Sam gave a little shudder, his breath coming slow and even. They lay there together, both suffering in their own different ways. But Jesse was Sam's father. He must set a good example for his son. To show him that he truly believed *Gott* rules over all. That no matter what trials came their way, they could overcome anything through faith and obedience to *Gott's* will. Surely the Lord hadn't abandoned them.

Or had He?

In the wee hours of the night, Sam finally slept. Jesse felt the boy's body soften, his little chest rising slowly with each breath. But there was no peace of mind for Jesse.

Ever so gently, he eased away from his son and stood looking down at the boy. Dried tears streaked Sam's pale cheeks. He looked so innocent. So pure and defenseless. And an overwhelming urge to protect him flooded Jesse with deep and abiding love. He was Sam's father and owed it to the boy to care for him. To help him any way he possibly could.

Sam shivered and Jesse reached to tug the covers higher over his child's slender shoulders. Turning, Jesse walked out of the room. The stairs creaked beneath his weight as he went to stoke the stove and warm up the house. Morning would be here soon. They'd get busy with their activities and it would ease the tension for a time…until nighttime fell and they once again were tortured by their painful memories.

He stared out the dark windows, seeing the faint golden light of sunrise. The mountains were beautiful here, reminding Jesse just how small and insig-

nificant he really was. And yet, he knew *Gott* loved
him. Surely He would care for him and Sam.

It was Church Sunday and he must soon awaken
his son for morning chores. They would drive seven
miles to Bishop Yoder's farm where they would listen to the Lord's word and worship *Gott*. That must
never change. Jesse's beliefs had become his anchor
in life. He could never abandon his faith. If he did,
he knew Alice wouldn't approve. She was counting
on him to teach Sam. To show their son how to be a
good man of faith.

Becca Graber would undoubtedly be at church
too. Maybe Jesse should speak with her about Sam.
Perhaps he should swallow his pride and ask the
pretty schoolteacher for advice. Maybe she had some
good ideas that might help Sam.

In the kitchen, Jesse sat on one of the hard,
wooden chairs he'd made with his own two hands.
Hours of working late into the night as he strived to
create a warm and welcoming place for him and Sam
to live. In the past, he had enjoyed such work. Especially when he showed his new creations to Alice.
She would smile with approval and reward him with
a gentle hug and kiss. Now, she wasn't here and he
wondered why he even tried. What did he have to
live for anymore?

Sam!

The boy's name came to his mind as if in a shout.
He must forgive and forget and keep striving to better serve others. As a father, he owed that to his little
boy. He owed it to Alice and to his *Gott* too. He must
not quit. Not now, not ever. The Savior would want

him to forgive and keep going. Surely Sam would start to talk again on his own. If they just left him alone, the boy would figure it out and speak again. Wouldn't he?

Feeling overwhelmed by his convictions, Jesse leaned forward and rested his elbows on his knees. He stared at the growing light of day until the sun became a golden ring of light and his eyes burned and his vision blurred. And then, as the grief washed over him in a fresh wave of pain, he bowed his head, cupped his face in his hands, and wept.

He was watching her again. Becca felt Jesse King's eyes on her even before she turned and looked at him. Sitting on the hard, backless bench, she tried to concentrate on what the minister was saying. It was Sunday morning, a bright, crisp day that was perfect for worship services. For several minutes, she focused on the preaching. Quoting Psalms 127, Jeremiah Beiler's voice was filled with emotion as he described children as a heritage from God who should be loved and cherished.

Looking up, Becca saw Jesse gazing intently at the minister. Jesse's forehead was furrowed in a slight frown, his eyes crinkled in thought. Hmm. Maybe he should remember that Sam should be valued instead of being brushed off as a bother.

At that moment, Jesse tilted his head and his eyes clashed, then locked with hers. She looked away, her face heating up with embarrassment. She'd encouraged him to let her help with Sam's speech problem and he'd refused. She'd do what she could for the boy during school hours but she couldn't force Jesse to listen to her. He had to take the next step. She just hoped that was soon before Sam was too old and set in his ways to start talking again.

"What's going on between you and Jesse King?" Naomi Fisher asked Becca later as they cleaned up after the noon meal.

Naomi was Becca's aunt and had helped her get this teaching position in Riverton. Knowing how Becca's heart had been broken by Vernon, Naomi had written her in January to ask if she might like to stay with her and work as the teacher until the school year ended in May. Longing for a chance to escape Vernon and Ruth's happy preparations for their marriage, Becca had jumped at the chance.

"What do you mean?" Becca asked.

Standing in the kitchen at the bishop's home, she washed another plate and set it in the dish drain. Aunt Naomi promptly picked it up to dry with a long, white cloth.

"I saw you two looking at each other during the meetings. You are lovely and he is a handsome widower. I'm not surprised he might be interested in you," Naomi said.

Becca snorted. "Believe me, Jesse King is far from interested. I've simply offered to assist Sam with his speaking problem and the man refuses to be helped."

Though she spoke low so the numerous other women working around them wouldn't hear her words, Becca couldn't prevent a note of irritation from entering her voice.

"I'm sure he's still hurting," Naomi said. "You know he lost his wife and two young daughters in a house fire a year ago."

"*Ja*, I know all about it. But it's no excuse to ignore Sam's needs," Becca said.

"*Ach*, did you also know it was Sam who started the fire?"

Becca gasped and turned to stare at her aunt. "*Ne*, I didn't know that. Are you sure?"

Naomi shrugged and set the clean plate aside before picking up another one to dry. "Since I wasn't there, I'm not sure of anything. But that's what Sarah Yoder said."

Sarah was the bishop's wife and would be privy to such private information like that.

"I'm surprised Sarah would tell you something so personal. It sounds like gossip to me," Becca whispered low.

Naomi drew her shoulders back, her expression filled with dignity. "She wasn't gossiping at all, I can assure you. I accidentally overheard her talking to Bishop Yoder about it right after Jesse and his son moved here to Riverton. She didn't know I was there listening and I haven't spoken about it since. I have only told you because you're my niece and I think the information might help you to resolve Sam's problem. The poor child. Losing his *mamm* and sisters so young. No wonder the little lamb doesn't speak. And no wonder Jesse is so sullen all the time. I feel bad for him, having to carry such a horrible burden on his shoulders."

Yes, no wonder. But knowing that Sam had started

the house fire changed everything and nothing. He still needed help. And soon. Was it possible that Jesse was angry with his son for starting the fire? Did Jesse hold a grudge against his own son? Oh, it was too cruel. No wonder Sam didn't speak. Knowing what he'd done, he must be wracked by guilt. And living with a father who blamed him for what happened must be more than Sam could bear. No doubt Jesse fought against his own guilt as well.

"Ahem, excuse me, ladies. I'm sorry to interrupt your work."

Becca looked up, surprised to see Jesse King standing in the open doorway to the kitchen. And for the umpteenth time that day, her face flamed hotter than a bonfire. Had he overheard her and Aunt Naomi talking about him? Did he know how curious she was?

The room went deathly quiet. Sarah Yoder stepped away from the gas-powered oven and nodded pleasantly. Since this was her home, she was their hostess and responsible to see that everyone was comfortable.

"*Hallo*, Jesse. What can we help you with?" she asked.

His gaze drifted past the sea of smiling faces until it landed on Becca.

"I was hoping to speak with Miss Graber for a moment," he said.

Someone gave a breathless laugh and Becca wished the floor would just open up and swallow her whole.

"It's about Sam," Jesse continued, as if sensing the other women's interest.

A pulse of energy shot up from Becca's toes. He wanted to talk to her about Sam. Maybe he was finally ready to make a plan with her to help the boy. Everyone knew she was the schoolteacher and that Sam didn't talk. Not even to his school friends. She was duty bound to help the child in any way possible. What could be more natural than for Jesse to want to confer with his son's teacher about the boy's problem? But Jesse's timing couldn't be worse. Becca hated the thought that everyone in her *Gmay* might think there was something romantic going on between them. Because there wasn't. No, not at all.

"Of course! I'd be happy to discuss Sam with you." Giving an efficient nod, she quickly dried her hands and set the towel aside.

As Becca made her way over to the door, Lizzie Stoltzfus and Abby Fisher, her cousin's wife, ducked their heads together to share a whispered comment. Even Julia Hostetler, who had been *Englisch* before her recent conversion and marriage into their faith, was grinning like a fool. Only old Marva Geingerich, who was almost ninety years old, was frowning with disapproval.

Had they all lost their minds? Becca had no romantic interest in Jesse King. None whatsoever. She hated the indifferent way he treated Sam. Even if he was handsome and tall as a church steeple, his brusque manner made it difficult for Becca to like him.

He lifted a hand for her to precede him as she

stepped out into the sunshine. As she stood beneath the barren branches of a tall elm tree, the frosty wind sent a shiver through her that made her gasp and wish she'd grabbed her warm shawl on her way outside. Before she knew what was happening, Jesse had doffed his warm frock coat and swept it over her trembling shoulders. She instantly caught his scent, a warm clean smell of hay, horses and peppermint. He was gazing at her lavender dress and she looked down, wondering if she had spilled something on it.

"That's a nice color on you. I'm sorry to bring you out here on such a cold day. I'll try not to keep you very long," he said.

She stared up at him, blinking in stunned amazement. All rational thought skipped right out of her head and she didn't know what to say. Had he actually paid her a compliment? Maybe her ears had deceived her. "I, um, *danke*, but that really isn't necessary."

She forced herself to hand his coat back to him. Though she really was freezing, a glance at the house told her that Aunt Naomi and Sarah Yoder were both staring out the kitchen window at her. To make matters worse, they had most certainly watched as Jesse offered her his coat. No doubt it would be all over the *Gmay* by early evening that she and Jesse King were an item. And having been the focus of romantic gossip back in Ohio, that was the last thing Becca wanted here in Colorado.

Seeing the smiling women at the window, Jesse inclined his head and seemed to understand her dilemma. "I'm sorry if I've created trouble for you.

That wasn't my intention. I only wanted to ask if you know what is wrong with Sam."

She folded her arms tightly as he put his coat back on. Licking her dry lips, she tried to concentrate on the subject at hand. "I'm not an expert but I believe he has what is called *selective mutism*."

She briefly explained what she knew about the disorder and that she didn't think Sam had any choice in the matter.

"His anxiety is so strong that he is literally scared silent. He's not trying to be rude or mean or cause you problems. He couldn't speak even if he wanted to," she said.

Jesse frowned. "You think he's too frightened to talk?"

She nodded. "Exactly. I know it must be a sensitive subject but I believe something about his mother and sisters' deaths has created so much apprehension in Sam that he literally cannot talk anymore."

Jesse looked down at the ground, scuffing one toe of his black boot against a small rock. "I was afraid of that. When I was in the library yesterday, I came across a couple of books on this topic but I haven't yet had the opportunity to read much about it. I was planning to start reading the book you checked out for me later this evening."

So. Maybe he really did want to help his son after all.

"From what I understand about the disorder, such children usually talk at home, where they feel more comfortable," she said. "But at school or in other social situations where they feel uncomfortable or nervous, they are silent. And punishing the child or making him feel guilty for not speaking would only exacerbate the problem."

Jesse's forehead curved in a deep scowl. "But Sam doesn't speak at home either."

He sounded so forlorn that Becca didn't have the heart to point out that Sam obviously didn't feel comfortable inside the walls of his own house. She figured that was possibly Jesse's fault. The boy must fear his own father. And whether that was because Sam felt guilt over his mother and sisters' deaths or for some other reason, Becca couldn't say.

"If you're amenable, there are a few techniques we can try to help Sam." She then launched into a rapid description of what those methods were. Last night, she'd done a lot of reading on the topic and put a great deal of thought into how they both might assist Sam with his problem. She'd even written up a plan of action last night. Things each of them might do to help Sam and techniques to measure Sam's improvement. She was eager to share her ideas with Jesse in detail and hoped he wouldn't refuse.

He listened politely to her explanations but made no comment.

"That all sounds like a huge time commitment on both our parts," he said.

She nodded. "*Ja*, it will take a lot of time. But I think Sam is worth it."

He hesitated, looking skeptical. "I do too but I'll have to think about it. I want to make sure I'm doing the right things for my *sohn*."

"I understand but I'd like to get started as soon as

possible. The longer we delay, the worse the situation might become. It would be ideal if Sam could stay an extra hour after school several days each week so I could work with him one-on-one," she said.

Jesse frowned. "Since I'm alone and have to pick up Sam from school, that might not be possible. I've got my hands full already. Couldn't you just send extra homework home with him? I can make sure he does it."

She shook her head, thinking Jesse didn't understand. "More homework won't help Sam talk. He needs some intense interaction with other people. He needs to feel comfortable around us so we can help him speak and we need to provide opportunities to teach him how to speak again."

Jesse stood there looking down at her, his eyes unblinking as he considered her ideas. She didn't interrupt, allowing him time to digest and mull it all over in his own mind.

"I understand what you're asking. Let me think about it. And *danke* for your help. I appreciate your efforts." Turning, he walked away, heading toward the barn where the other men were lounging and visiting after their noon meal. Bishop Yoder and *Dawdi* Zeke hailed him over.

And just like that, Jesse was gone. Becca longed to call him back or chase after him to make him agree to her proposal. But something held her back. She felt almost desperate to help Sam. As if an unknown force were pushing her forward and her future happiness depended on it. But Jesse would have to decide. And she resolved then to offer a prayer to *Gott* that Jesse made the right decision.

Chapter Four

Becca set the last plate from supper into the dish drain. Sinking her hands into the hot, soapy water, she rinsed out the dishcloth before wiping down the counters and kitchen table. Supper was finally finished. *Dawdi* Zeke and Jakob were out in the barn finishing the evening chores. It was Monday evening and her mind whirled with all the lesson plans she still needed to review before school in the morning. Maybe she could grade some papers during recess tomorrow. And then she needed to assign some readings for the scholars to memorize for the end-of-year program. So much to do.

"Have you spoken to Bishop Yoder about Caleb's behavior at school, yet?" Aunt Naomi picked up a glass to dry off with a dish towel.

Becca slid the butter dish inside the gas-powered fridge, giving an absentminded shake of her head. She had explained in detail the troubles she was having at school. "*Ne*, I'm not even sure he's the culprit. I have no proof, just an instinct that he's the instigator. I've already separated him and Enos Albrecht. When the two of them sat together, they seemed to egg each other on. Besides, what *gut* would it do to tell their *eldre*? The bishop would just think I can't control the school."

Abby Fisher, Jakob's wife, stood across the room, cleaning and sorting the eggs Becca had helped her gather before dinner. Becca knew they would sell the eggs in town to help supplement their household income.

"It might help to tell them what's going on. Then they could speak with their sons," Abby said.

"*Ja*, the bishop wants the school to succeed," Naomi added. "Especially since Caroline was injured in that horrible buggy accident last month. Without a teacher, we feared we'd have to send our *kinder* to the *Englisch* schools. It's a blessing you were able to *komm* here so quickly. I'm sure Bishop Yoder would be mortified to know that one of his own *kinder* is causing so much trouble."

Becca understood very well why the Amish didn't want to send their children to the *Englisch* schools. She listened to her aunt's advice, thinking over what she said. In the short time she had lived in this home, she'd become quite close to these two women and she valued their opinions. But maybe she wasn't cut out to be a teacher. Though she enjoyed her profession, maybe she had made a mistake by coming here to Colorado. If she couldn't even control her school, she wouldn't be able to make teaching a lifelong career.

"I hope Reuben hasn't been participating in any

shenanigans." Abby looked at Becca and paused, her forehead creased with concern.

"*Ne*, he's been *gut* as gold. In fact, he tried to stop the trouble last week when I pulled the toy snake out of my desk drawer," Becca said.

Naomi showed a relieved smile. "*Gut*! There was a time when Abby first came to live with us that I was mighty worried about his behavior."

"*Ja*, I remember when I first came to live here, he put cracker crumbs between my bedsheets and dirt in my shoes." Abby laughed at the reminder.

Becca gasped, hardly able to believe her cousin's sweet, polite ten-year-old son would do such a thing. "*Behiedes*? He actually did that?"

Abby nodded. "He certainly did."

"But why?"

Abby shrugged. "He felt threatened by me. He thought I was trying to take his *mudder's* place after she had died."

Becca could hardly imagine Reuben being so obnoxious. Now, Abby was Reuben's new stepmother and they seemed to love each other very much. Becca just hoped Caleb and Enos didn't try such mischief on her.

"What did you do to get Reuben to stop?" she asked.

A smile curved Abby's lips, as if she were remembering something good. "I put uplifting notes in his lunch pail every day for school. He hated it at first, because the notes were from me. But finally, I convinced him I wasn't trying to usurp his *mamm's* place and I just wanted to be his friend. It took time to convince Jakob as well."

"Jakob?" Becca had known her cousin was brokenhearted when his first wife died in childbirth but she hadn't known he'd been resistant to the idea of marrying Abby.

"*Ja*, he wanted nothing to do with me, at first."

Becca snorted. "I can hardly believe that. You're so *wundervoll*. What man wouldn't want to marry you? Besides, he's obviously crazy in love with you now."

Leaning her hip against the counter, Abby paused in her chore, holding a white egg aloft as she glanced at Becca. "*Ach*, he didn't always love me. It was a very uncomfortable situation. Here I was, living in a strange place, thinking he had proposed marriage, only to discover that it had been his *vadder's* idea and Jakob knew nothing about it."

"Hmm. That would be difficult. I doubt uplifting notes will work on Caleb and Enos, though," Becca said.

"But a stern talk from their *vadders* might do the job." Naomi lifted her eyebrows in a severe expression to make her point.

"I'm not so sure. Caleb's older brother and sister have been getting after him for some of the tricks he pulls and I suspect they've already told the bishop what's going on. Yet, Caleb continues to misbehave. Tomorrow, we'll start practicing songs and readings for the end-of-year program. Maybe if I ask for their help, Caleb and Enos might become vested in the school's success. I might even ask Caleb to start reading with Sam King. Maybe if Caleb feels needed, he'll behave better."

Abby slid a carton of cleaned eggs into the refrigerator. "*Ja*, that might help. You are very wise. Is little Sam still not speaking?"

Becca released a pensive sigh. "*Ne*, and I'm quite worried about him. His *vadder* doesn't seem concerned at all. He said he thinks Sam will start speaking on his own when he's *gut* and ready."

"But you don't agree?" Naomi sat at the table and folded clean laundry from a basket resting on the floor.

"*Ne*, I don't." Becca spoke rather harshly, trying not to feel angry at Jesse's neglect of his son. But it still rankled her that he seemed a bit insensitive to Sam's needs. "Jesse King is an odious, contrary man. I realize he's lost a lot and been hurt but he should set aside his own pain and put his *sohn's* needs first. I think Sam is suffering badly from the trauma of his *mudder* and *schweschdere's* deaths."

A thud and then the sound of the front door opening came from the living room. Becca figured the men must have finished their evening chores.

"*Ach*, the poor dear," Abby cooed in a sympathetic tone. "And his poor *vadder* too. What a horrible thing for both of them to go through. I know how hard it was for Reuben and Ruby to lose their *mamm*. I don't think they'll ever get over the shock. And neither will Jakob. Sam is blessed to have you to comfort him."

Becca didn't agree. She didn't know what to do for the little boy. How she wished she were more experienced and knew more about special needs like Sam's. But her eighth-grade education didn't provide much insight on such things. The boy was obviously traumatized. Perhaps Jesse was too. And right now, she felt as though she were the blind leading the blind.

"*Ach*, what that little boy needs is a *mudder*. And Jesse needs a *frau*. It would do them both a world of *gut* if Jesse were to remarry," Naomi said.

Maybe so but Becca wasn't in the running for either role. Not after the way Vernon had broken her heart. She couldn't even think about marriage now. Not without feeling nauscous and trembly all over.

"I've heard Jesse has already made a huge difference at that run-down farm he purchased. Jakob drives by there almost every day and said he can see improvements already. And you must have noticed he's quite a handsome *mann*," Abby said.

Of course Becca had noticed. She'd have to be dead or blind not to. But that didn't matter. Not to her. Vernon had been good-looking too, but he'd turned out to be disingenuous. She'd rather marry an earnest, hardworking man who loved the Lord as much as he loved her than be shackled to a handsome, shallow man who didn't really cherish her.

"I'm not interested. I'm simply his *sohn's* teacher and nothing more," she insisted.

She slid into a chair and reached to help fold the socks. As she did so, she felt Naomi's gaze resting on her like a ten-ton sledge. She didn't look up, hoping the older woman didn't notice her flaming cheeks.

"Becca?"

All three women looked up in unison. Jakob stood

in the doorway, still wearing his heavy winter coat and black felt hat. He'd obviously just come in from the barn.

"There's someone here to see you," he said.

She tilted her head, thinking it quite late for an evening caller. "Who is it?"

Jakob lowered his head, but kept his gaze pinned on her. "Jesse King."

Becca went very still. Her heart skipped a beat, then sped into triple time. What on earth was Jesse doing here at this late hour?

Jesse waited patiently for Becca to appear. Standing just inside the closed front door, he held his hat between his hands and gazed at the clock on the wall. He was grateful to get his son out of the cold night air. Sam fidgeted nervously beside him, his eyes wide and filled with apprehension.

This was a nice, spacious living room, with a huge rag rug covering the wooden floor, a plain but comfy-looking sofa, two soft chairs, a simple but serviceable coffee table, and a rocking chair. A set of brown curtains covered the dark, cold windows. The walls were painted white, clean but simple. A black woodburning stove sat near the central wall, emanating enough heat to warm the entire house. It felt nice and cozy in this home. The way he wished his house could be. With time, he hoped he could make a comfortable place for him and Sam to live again. But they'd always be lonely.

Dawdi Zeke beckoned to Sam, enticing the boy to sit on the couch beside him. The elderly man held out a piece of peppermint candy. Sam took it into his hand but didn't say thank you.

A subtle movement across the room caused Jesse to lift his head. Becca Graber stood there, wiping her hands on her apron. Jakob stood behind her with his wife and mother. Jesse could see the curiosity in their eyes. As a new widower, he was highly aware of his marriage eligibility. In fact, Bishop Yoder had just reminded him at church that they had several attractive young women in the *Gmay* who needed husbands. Becca was one of them. But Jesse wasn't interested. He knew as an Amish man that it was his duty to remarry and bring more children into the world. To work and live and raise a good *familye* who loved *Gott*. But Jesse didn't want to marry again. He couldn't even think about replacing Alice. Not when his love for her was still so strong.

Naomi Fisher eyed him like a hawk eyed a field mouse. He knew they were all wondering what he was doing here. It was already dark outside and he should be home, putting Sam to bed. In a glance, Jesse took in Becca's flushed cheeks, startling blue eyes and flustered expression. Tendrils of golden hair had escaped her *kapp*. She looked beautiful and a warning tingle slid down the column of his spine. All his senses ratcheted into high alert and his common sense told him to leave right now.

Becca stepped over to one of the soft chairs and sat down before smoothing her apron over her knees. "Mr. King, what can I do for you?"

Here it was. The big question.

Jakob and Abby still hovered near the open doorway with *Dawdi* Zeke still on the couch, and Jesse was suddenly at a loss for words. They could hear everything. Maybe he shouldn't have come here. Maybe he should have waited to speak with Becca until he picked Sam up from school tomorrow afternoon. But he feared by then he would have lost his courage.

He cleared his throat. "Miss Graber, I'm sorry for the interruption. I was hoping I could speak with you for just a few minutes about Sam. In private, please."

Okay, he'd gotten that much out. But his words caused another stir as Jakob and the other two women sought to move away from the doorway.

"I'll see if Reuben and Ruby are ready for bed yet." Abby climbed the stairs, her skirts swishing as she went.

"And I better go read them a bedtime story," Jakob said, following after his wife.

Dawdi Zeke came to his feet with a bit of difficulty and took Sam's hand.

"How about if you and I go see if there's any apple pie left over from supper?" The elderly man spoke to the boy as he hobbled toward the kitchen.

Sam went with the elderly man. He didn't speak but his eyes sparkled and he nodded eagerly. Jesse wasn't surprised. With Alice gone, they rarely enjoyed anything sweet at home. A slice of pie would be a real treat for the child. Even Jesse's mouth watered at the thought.

Naomi welcomed the boy into her kitchen with a cheery voice. "*Hallo*, Samuel. There's plenty of pie to eat. Have you had your supper yet?"

Sam nodded but Jesse knew his son could eat again. The cold beans and burnt corn bread Jesse had prepared earlier hadn't done much to appease either of their appetites. Their stomachs were full but the meal had left a lot to be desired.

"*Ach*, and how about if I send an apple pie home with you and your *vadder* to enjoy tomorrow? You can eat it at your leisure and have some left over for the next day too," Naomi said.

Jesse almost smiled at that but didn't want to betray his eagerness. At this point, an apple pie seemed like a feast. This house smelled of pine needles and a delicious supper and his stomach rumbled in spite of having already eaten.

"Won't you sit down?" Becca invited with a lift of her hand.

He sat opposite her on the sofa, perched there as he set his hat on the coffee table. She folded her hands primly in her lap, her blue eyes unblinking as she gazed at him expectantly.

"*Ach*, so what did you want to speak with me about?" Her voice sounded calm and soothing, not at all perturbed by his unexpected visit.

Here it was. He didn't know what to say. He didn't move or breathe. Afraid to upset her. Afraid she'd say no. After all, he'd been rather rude to her in the past. Maybe he'd already burned his bridges with this woman. Maybe her offer to help him with Sam was gone.

"Ahem, I… I've been thinking about what you've suggested, with Sam. I mean, I've been reading the book you checked out for me and realize his problem isn't going away anytime soon."

He paused, taking a deep breath as he tried to gather his thoughts. She inclined her head but waited patiently, her gaze never leaving his face.

"I don't want Sam to grow up and not be able to speak," he continued. "I want him to have a *gut* future. I'm at my wits' end and don't know what to do to help him. Please. Will you work with him?"

There. He'd gotten his request out in one long breath. He hated to beg but that's what he'd do if it meant Sam could talk and be normal again.

"I would love to help," she said immediately.

It took a moment for his mind to digest what she'd said. And when he did, her words put him instantly at ease.

"You would?" He could hardly believe it. He was beyond relieved.

"*Ja*, you already know I'm not an expert in this area, so I can't make any promises. But I'll do the best I can to help Sam," she said.

He released a pensive sigh, only just realizing that he'd been holding his breath. A huge weight seemed to fall off his shoulders. Finally. Finally he could stop fighting it and get some help.

"*Danke*. I'm so grateful," he said.

"So I can understand what happened, can you give me a little background on Sam's situation?" she asked.

Memories flooded Jesse's mind. He didn't want to talk about this but knew Becca needed to know a few details if she were to help Sam.

"I… I was a certified firefighter where we lived in Pennsylvania," he said in an aching whisper, the memories making him shake like a newborn colt. "I was called out on another house fire and wasn't there when my own home caught fire. When I got home in the early morning hours, I tried to save my *familye* but I was too late." He looked down and saw the scars on his hands and arms. They were still there, reminding him of his failure. "I found Sam up in the hayloft, curled in a fetal position. When I asked him what happened, he became hysterical. All he would say was that he was sorry and it was his fault. Two days later, we buried my *frau* and *dechder*. Sam hasn't spoken a word since the funeral."

Becca winced. "I'm so very sorry for your loss."

Her words made no difference but her soft, compassionate voice seemed to ease the ache just a bit. Even though it had been a year, the tale still rattled Jesse's nerves. He'd lost almost everything that horrible day. Now, all he had left was Sam. And he knew, no matter what, he had to help his little boy. Alice would expect nothing less.

Becca stood abruptly. "Wait here. I'll be right back."

The wooden steps creaked as she went up the stairs to the second story. She returned moments later carrying a booklet and several pieces of paper, which she handed to him.

"This is a copy of an intervention plan I've already drawn up for Sam," she said. "Just a few simple steps on how we can offer positive reinforcement, some stimulus fading techniques to desensitize him when he's around other people, ways to help him build social skills, and tactics so he won't feel as anxious. If you'll read through these materials and try to incorporate them at home, I think we can help him overcome this problem. I'll do the same at school, only much more since he'll be with his classmates during that time."

Jesse glanced at the plan of action, surprised at how detailed it was. It was quite thorough and easy to follow with step-by-step instructions dealing with a variety of scenarios. For the first time in a year, a lance of optimism speared his chest with hope. He wasn't surprised to see that she'd assigned him to read with Sam each night. No matter how busy he was right now, he had no excuses. If nothing else, spending more time with Sam might increase his bond with the boy. And after what they'd been through, they both needed time together more than anything.

"*Ja*, I will do these things. I'll read to him each night," he promised.

Her shoulders relaxed and he realized she'd been tensed, expecting him to refuse again.

"That's *wundervoll*," she exclaimed, her smile so bright that he had to swallow. "And I'd like to suggest one more thing that I hope will help all of us."

He quirked one eyebrow and waited. It wasn't until she spoke again that he realized he was holding his breath.

"I think Sam needs extra tutoring, to help with his school studies. Since you live only a short way up the road, I propose that I bring Sam home from

school every Monday, Wednesday and Friday afternoon. Then I can tutor him for an extra hour or so.
And the added benefit is that you won't have to pick
him up on those days, which should alleviate your
workload too. Since today is Monday, I'd like to start
tutoring him tomorrow, even though it's Tuesday.
Does that sound all right?"

Jesse just stared, his mind struggling to absorb
what she'd suggested. It was true that the Fisher farm
wasn't far away from his place. In the darkest part
of the night, he could even see their lights gleaming
across his fields. They were his neighbors, though
he hadn't developed a very close friendship with
them yet. He just hadn't had the time for the nice-
ties. Maybe later in the summer, after his fields were
planted, he could do something about that.

"*Ja*, that would work fine," he said, suddenly willing to agree to anything she wanted.

Actually, her proposal would be an unexpected
blessing. Living so far outside of town provided the
quiet and solitude he desired but it also meant he had
to take Sam to school early in the mornings and fetch
him home in the afternoons. Some days, that posed
a great hardship, depending on what he was working on. He did it because he believed an education
was so important for Sam and because he loved his
son. But it hadn't been easy.

"*Fie*. We'll start with the tutoring tomorrow and
go from there." She smiled and came to her feet, signaling they were finished.

He stood slowly. As she stepped over to the
kitchen and invited him in for a huge slice of pie, he

felt like he was moving in a fog. Naomi and *Dawdi* Zeke welcomed him. They laughed and chatted as though he were a member of their *familye*. Jesse didn't say much but nodded and smiled in return. It felt so mundane and normal and he appreciated their kindness more than he could say. His gaze kept roaming over to Becca as she offered Sam a chilled glass of milk. The child smiled and chewed with relish. And that's when something dawned on Jesse. He hadn't seen his son look this happy since before the house fire. Already, Becca had made a huge difference in Sam's life.

By the time Jesse loaded his sleepy son into their buggy for the short drive home, he couldn't help thinking that his *familye* used to be fun like this. They used to laugh and talk and eat pie together around the kitchen table. Oh, how he missed them all. How he missed the love and companionship they used to share.

How he missed Alice.

He had Becca to thank for today. She was so dynamic and outspoken, but also kind and generous. Because she was Sam's teacher, she seemed to think she was entitled to make demands on Jesse and his time. The most irksome part was that she was right. Sam needed help. His father's help.

Becca was pushy, insistent and giving. She was so different from his gentle, quiet, submissive Alice. Jesse just hoped Becca's plan worked and Sam would soon start talking again. And as he drove them home through the cold night air, all of a sudden the world seemed to be filled with amazing possibilities.

Chapter Five

The following morning, Sam didn't show up for school. They'd had another bad snowstorm in the night, so Becca thought perhaps Jesse couldn't get his horse and buggy through the tall drifts that covered the dirt road leading from his farm. Since she lived just one mile away from his place, she knew the plows had been out early that morning to clear the county roads so the school buses with the *Englisch* kids could get to school safely. And that benefited the Amish too. But each farm had a dirt road that extended quite a way down and no one plowed that for them. Maybe tonight, she'd suggest to Jakob that he take his horses and sleigh over to Jesse's place to help clear his driveway and road.

Two hours into the school day, she was standing in front of the chalkboard, helping the fourth-graders work through some particularly difficult arithmetic problems. The front door suddenly blasted open with a gust of chilly air. Becca whirled around and saw little Sam standing there with his father. Both of them were bundled up in heavy black coats, boots, knit caps, gloves and scarfs. While Jesse closed the door, the boy hurried over to the coatracks where he doffed his winter wear and hung it up. A quick glance at the other first-graders told him what subject they were working on as he slid into his seat and took out his penmanship book. And that's when Becca saw his red eyes and tearstained face. The boy had obviously been crying. But why? What was the matter?

"I'm sorry we're late. It couldn't be helped." Jesse lifted a hand as he spoke in *Deitsch*.

Under normal circumstances, Becca would have just smiled and welcomed Jesse and Sam to school. But the fact that Sam had been crying upset her. Setting the chalk aside, she walked over to Jesse and indicated she'd like him to accompany her outside where they could speak in private.

"Continue with your studies, please," she called to the scholars before shutting the door against intrusion.

Standing on the front step, she faced Jesse, her emotions a riot of unease. "What has happened? Why is Sam so late?"

It was only when he responded that she realized she had also spoken in *Deitsch*. His and Sam's sudden appearance had flustered her more than she liked to admit.

Jesse shrugged, not meeting her gaze. "Sam had a bad morning. He is all right now."

"Are you sure? He looks distressed." She spoke in *Englisch* this time, trying to remain professional.

"*Ja*, he is fine now."

Hmm. His comment led her to believe it wasn't the heavy drifts of snow that had caused Sam to cry. So, what had happened?

"Are you sure you're up to bringing him home this afternoon after school? We got nine inches out at our place and I don't want you stranded on the road somewhere," Jesse said.

He acted like everything was completely normal, which confused her even more. Little six-year-old boys didn't cry for no reason. Maybe she could find out what was the matter from Sam, although that might prove difficult since the boy didn't talk.

"*Ja*, the sky is clear and the snow is melting now," she said. "We shouldn't have any more storms for several days. I should be able to bring Sam home and tutor him this afternoon without any problems."

"*Gut*, I'll see you then. I'll watch for you and *komm* looking for you if you're late arriving at my place."

His words gave her a bit of comfort. It was nice to know someone was looking out for her in case she had trouble with her horse and buggy.

Jesse turned and walked down the steps, his long legs moving fast as he stepped around muddy areas where the snow had melted into puddles.

Rubbing her arms against the frigid air, Becca didn't call him back or question him further. She had no right to interfere.

She returned to the classroom and discovered that the students hadn't made much progress without her help. Lenore Schwartz, an eighth-grader, had just stepped in to offer assistance. With Becca's arrival,

Lenore handed over the piece of chalk and returned to her desk.

"Thank you, Lenore," Becca called after the girl in a pleasant voice.

"You're *willkomm*." The girl nodded and smiled shyly.

Becca could tell some of the scholars were becoming more relaxed around her. After all, this was only her sixth day of teaching these kids. She was delighted to know they were starting to feel comfortable enough to step in and help the younger children.

"Let's see, where are we?" Pressing a finger to her lips, Becca stepped up to the chalkboard and studied the problem once more.

She glanced at Susan Hostetler, one of the fourth-graders who was working this particular problem. Becca pointed at a specific area of the addition. "I think you're getting hung up right here."

"*Ach*, I told you so. You're adding it wrong." Caleb Yoder spoke with impatience.

Since Caleb was her only fifth-grader, she had brought him in to work with the fourth-graders. He brushed past Susan, picked up a piece of chalk and started to work her problem. Becca intervened, quickly erasing what he had written on the board.

"Caleb, this is Susan's problem to work out. Please wait patiently for your turn," she said.

The other children frowned with disapproval at Caleb's rude behavior and he stepped back with a huff. Becca was glad. Maybe peer pressure would help keep Caleb in line.

Becca faced Susan again. "Did you remember to carry the nine?"

For several moments, Susan stared at the chalkboard, her forehead knitted in a deep frown of concentration. Then, the light clicked on inside her brain and she gasped in comprehension. "*Ach*, it's right here!"

The girl quickly worked the problem, wrote the answer below, then turned to face Becca with an expectant smile. "Is it right this time? Is it?"

Becca nodded, showing a wide smile of approval. "You are absolutely correct. Well done!"

"Yay!" the girl cried, her face wide with a happy smile.

A laugh broke from Becca's throat. She loved this part of teaching. When she saw the light of knowledge glimmer in one of her student's eyes, it made her happy too. Yesterday, she'd doubted herself so much. But maybe she could do this after all. Once again, a part of her couldn't help wishing she could marry and have a *familye* of her own. Since Vernon had broken her heart, it wasn't to be. After the way he'd treated her, she didn't think she could trust another man ever again. And moping about her shattered dreams wouldn't do her any good. She had better get on with her life and make the best of it. But successes like this brought her a great deal of satisfaction and joy.

"Very well done," she praised Susan again, then glanced at Caleb. "I think you're a bit too advanced for these problems. You'll need a more difficult fraction to add."

She could tell her words pleased him. Praise usually brought on *Hochmut*, the pride of the world, so it wasn't encouraged among the Amish. But Becca thought a small compliment might help Caleb in this situation. While he watched her quizzically, she quickly wrote out a more strenuous problem with multiple fractions. Then, she handed her piece of chalk to him and stepped back to give him room to work.

He pressed his tongue to his upper lip while he studied the equation. Within moments, he had solved the problem with very little hesitation. He was definitely a bright scholar. Maybe that was the reason he kept getting into trouble. He was bored.

Well, she would just have to give him more work to do.

"Yay!" the other children called, quick to forgive him for being discourteous and quick to offer encouragement.

Becca laid a hand on Caleb's shoulder and met his eyes. "Very well done, Caleb. In fact, I think you are advanced enough that you should start helping one of the younger children with their arithmetic. How would you like to become Sam's math partner?"

Caleb glanced at the little boy, who sat quietly studying at his desk. A frown curved Caleb's mouth downward and Becca feared he might refuse.

"You know he doesn't speak, but you're such a *gut* student that I know you can explain things to him." Becca whispered the words for Caleb's ears alone. After all, she didn't want to hurt Sam's feelings. "You're quite a bit older and Sam really looks up to you. I'm sure he'd appreciate your help. And I'd love to tell your *vadder* that you're one of our school tutors."

A flicker of delight blazed in Caleb's eyes. He liked that. A lot.

"But you mustn't do Sam's work for him," she cautioned, still speaking softly so the other kids wouldn't overhear. "Just help show him where he might be getting the problems wrong and let him figure things out himself. Then we'll tell everyone what a *gut* tutor he has."

That did the trick. Caleb nodded and immediately went over to sit close to Sam and help with his simple addition. Caleb sat up straight, his movements filled with confidence. And Becca knew she'd done a good thing. Caleb was very bright and getting too bored, which led to him causing trouble in the school. But elevating him to tutor would help him focus more on helping Sam. It would help him concentrate on helping someone else instead of getting into trouble. Caleb would now be Sam's protector instead of his tormentor.

Feeling good about her day of teaching, Becca returned to her work with the other scholars and the morning whizzed by way too fast. She felt happy inside, knowing she'd just resolved a huge problem with Caleb. It made her glad she was a teacher. Glad she had come here to Colorado.

"Teacher Becca?"

She looked up and saw Karen Yoder holding her hand high in the air.

"Yes, Karen?" she said.

Karen indicated the clock on the wall. "It's lunchtime, teacher. I thought you might be too busy to notice."

Glancing at the clock, Becca gasped and realized her mistake. It was already eleven thirty. Where had the morning gone?

"Thank you, Karen. Scholars, please return to your desks and stand while we say our prayer of thanks," she said.

The children at the chalkboard returned to their seats and all the students stood while they recited in unison. When they finished, the scholars each gathered their lunch pails and congregated in several huddles to eat.

"When you're finished with your lunch, you're welcome to go outside and build a snowman. Or if it's too cold and you prefer to stay inside, feel free to get out the game boards and play quietly together," Becca told them.

The kids nodded, speaking in muted voices, an occasional laugh piercing the air. None of them went outside today. They stayed inside and played games instead.

Becca sat at her desk, putting the finishing touches on the end-of-year program while she took bites of her ham sandwich. And that's when she looked up and saw something amazing. Instead of teasing the younger boys, Caleb had invited little Sam and Andy over to join him and the older boys in a game of Life on the Farm. Sam didn't speak but he participated silently and smiled when he did something right. The other children encouraged him, acting the way she expected them to.

Becca smiled to herself, realizing maybe she could be a good teacher after all. Last week, she'd felt as though she were a failure. That she never should have come to Colorado. But what she had done with Caleb Yoder had been a big achievement. Maybe she could make it as a teacher after all.

Now, if she could just figure out how to help Sam speak again, she would be truly happy. This afternoon, she would drive the little boy home and offer him some tutoring. She'd be sure to spend a little extra time bouncing ideas off Jesse as to how to help his son as well. She prayed that he wouldn't resist and would take her advice well. And maybe during their conversation, she could find out what had caused Sam to cry that morning. She just hoped Jesse hadn't been cruel to his son. She liked Jesse. She really did. She just wished he was more sensitive to his son's needs.

By four o'clock that afternoon, Becca and Sam hadn't arrived at the house and Jesse was ready to go find them. He stumbled on his way out of the back shed and headed toward the barn. Even though it was still early, the sky was overcast with a cluster of gray clouds. Maybe the roads had iced up already. It was certainly cold enough. He didn't know how good a driver Becca was and started to worry.

He led Jimmy, his road horse, out of the barn. Taking a deep inhale of fresh air, he tried to clear his muddled mind. A blaze of panic almost overtook him. The horrible feeling of being out of control and losing everything that was good in life. And he couldn't do a single thing to stop it from happening. Maybe Becca hadn't been paying attention and went off the road. Maybe she and Sam were lying hurt somewhere in a ditch...

The jingle of a harness brought his attention and he looked up. Becca's horse and buggy pulled into the graveled yard. Jesse saw her and his son sitting on the front seat, both of them bundled up against the frigid air. Becca held the leather lead lines with her gloved hands, seeming alert and attentive as she drove with confidence.

"*Danke*, Lord. *Danke* for bringing them home safe." Jesse whispered the prayer of gratitude beneath his breath.

They were here. He could stop worrying. At least until Becca had to drive to her farm in an hour or so.

"*Hallo!*" she called as she hopped out of the buggy.

She reached back to help Sam down. The boy rested his little hands on her shoulders without hesitation. And that's when Jesse noticed his son seemed to trust his teacher quite a bit.

"Were you going somewhere?" she asked, looking at his horse as they walked over to greet him. Her blue eyes were bright and alive, her cheeks and nose pink from the chilled temperatures. He could see each of her exhales like a puff of smoke on the frosty air. And looped over one arm, she carried a rather large basket covered by a clean cloth. Probably her school books for tutoring Sam.

He nodded, leaning against Jimmy's front shoulder. For some reason, he felt extra tired today, though he'd never admit it to Becca. "*Ja*, I was getting ready to go and find you. Now that you're here, I'll put your horse in the barn until you're ready to leave."

Without being asked, Sam helped his father. Becca stood near the wide double doors, watching silently as they stabled her horse and offered it some water.

"It's barely four o'clock," she said. "I don't know why you were getting ready to *komm* and find us. School gets out at three thirty and I had to make sure all the scholars were picked up by their *eldre* and secure the building before I could leave…"

He turned to face her and her eyes widened and she gasped. "Jesse! What happened to you?"

Feeling confused, he reached up and touched his forehead where he discovered a giant bump forming there.

"It's nothing. I was working to repair one of the walls in the back shed and took a fall off the ladder a little while ago." He reached for the halter to lead Jimmy back inside the warm barn too.

Becca and Sam followed after him. The boy didn't speak but took hold of his father's elbow, his face creased with concern. Jesse could tell Sam was worried about him.

"Geht es dir gut?" Becca asked.

"*Ja*, I'm all right," he reassured them both. "The fall just knocked the wind out of me. I didn't realize I'd hit my head until just now."

He released Jimmy back into his stall and shut the

door. No wonder he had a mild headache and had been disoriented a few minutes earlier. But now, he could feel his mind clearing and realized he'd been stunned by the fall.

"Let's go inside the house. It's too cold out here," Becca said.

She still looked anxious and for some crazy reason that touched Jesse's heart like nothing else could. It had been a long time since someone had fretted and cared about him.

Even though he still had cows to milk and chickens to feed, he didn't argue with her. He wanted something warm to drink and then he'd finish his evening chores.

They went inside the back door, the warmth of the potbellied stove engulfing them. Though this house and the surrounding corrals and outbuildings needed tons of repairs, at least the old stove worked well as long as he kept it supplied with fuel.

Becca set her basket on the table and doffed her gloves and heavy shawl. She helped Sam do the same, tossing his hat and coat carelessly on a chair. While Becca went to the kitchen cupboards, Jesse placed more wood on the fire. When he set the kettle on the stove to heat up, he glanced over and saw Becca retrieving a clean dishcloth from a drawer. Thankfully, she didn't say a word about the sink filled with dirty dishes. He planned to wash them later tonight but knew his home suffered from his lack of tidiness. Alice had always kept their place immaculate and in good order. But with all the work he had to do just to get ready for spring planting, he couldn't seem to keep up with everything.

He didn't question Becca when she went outside to fill the dishcloth with small chunks of ice. By the time she'd returned, he had sat down to rest a moment. Without a word, she promptly placed the cold cloth over his forehead. He flinched and she moved more gently, her fingertips warm against his skin.

"Hold this against your head for a few minutes. It'll help the swelling go down," she said.

"I don't need this," he said.

"*Ja*, you do," she insisted. "I'm wondering if I should take you to see Eli Stoltzfus. He can tell if you need to go to the hospital in town."

Jesse had met Eli and knew the man was a certified paramedic who worked for the small hospital in Riverton. Since Jesse was a firefighter, he wasn't surprised to find an Amish paramedic here. He knew they never drove any automotive vehicles, but the Amish had quickly discovered the benefits of having EMTs, paramedics and firefighters among them.

"I don't need to see Eli. It's just a little bump on the head and I feel fine," he said.

Her forehead crinkled slightly but she didn't argue as she bustled over to the table and began emptying the contents of the basket she'd brought. Watching her, he couldn't help thinking she had a way of taking over his home every time she arrived. And yet, he didn't mind. Not really. Because she seemed to bring lots of comfort and order with her. But he was surprised when she removed a casserole dish, a loaf of homemade bread and a cherry pie from her basket.

His mouth watered at the sight of so much good food. His hunger alone told him that his head was okay. "What are those for?"

She didn't look up as she slid the casserole into the gas-powered oven and turned it on. It looked like some kind of pasta, cheese and hamburger mixture that smelled delicious. Simple but filling food that made his stomach rumble. Sam had homed in on the pie, climbing up on a chair so he could gaze longingly at the golden crust and plump red berries that had oozed out of the lattice top when it was baked.

"This is for your supper," she said. "It was easy to keep the food chilled until we got here and I figured you were busy and might appreciate a night off from cooking."

He laughed out loud. He couldn't help himself. "Is this your polite way of letting me know I'm a lousy cook?"

She laughed too, the sound high and sweet, her eyes sparkling with pleasure. "*Ach*, I don't mean to offend but you must admit that you really are a poor cook."

He nodded without argument, still smiling at her sense of humor. "I'm willing to concede your point and will admit I have come to dread meal preparation. I think Sam dreads it too."

Her smile stayed firmly in place as she removed several books from the bottom of the basket. "And these are for my tutoring session with Sam."

She handed the boy one book, which he took readily. A feeling of deep and abiding gratitude for her thoughtfulness rested over Jesse like a warm blan-

ket. And that's when he realized something important. He had laughed just a few moments ago. A loud,
full-bodied laugh that came from deep inside. It was
the first since Alice and his little girls had died. And
that made Jesse pause in startled wonder. He felt suddenly unfaithful to their memory. Disloyal for feeling happy when they were gone.

He stood abruptly and tossed the dishrag onto the
cupboard. "This is fine now. I've got chores to do."

Placing his black felt hat on his head, he closed
the door firmly behind him and hurried to the barn.
After tossing hay to the animals, he fed the chickens and milked the cow. The work gave him time to
gather his thoughts. To remember who he was and
what he was doing here.

Becca was efficient, bossy and wonderful but she
wasn't Alice. And he was not going to let her take
over his life or his thoughts. In his heart, he was still
a married man who was faithful to his wife. And he
wouldn't allow himself to be taken in by Becca's
competent ways.

Thirty minutes later, he returned to the kitchen,
carrying a bucket of frothy white milk. As he set it
on the table, he could hear Becca in the living room,
reading to Sam. He stepped over to the doorway and
peeked into the room without revealing his presence.
They both sat huddled together in the new rocking
chair he had finished making last night. Little by
little, he was getting things done but he was impatient to paint the ugly, scarred walls inside his home.
However, that would have to wait. There were more
pressing issues he needed to tend to right now or

they wouldn't have a livelihood. Issues such as getting the corrals and sheds repaired so he could buy livestock for their farm.

He listened silently as Becca read Sam a story about a cat named Elmo and a dog named Patches. The feline played a lot of tricks on the dog and got away with all sorts of antics. Finally, Becca finished the story with a laugh.

"I really like Elmo. He's so funny. He's always sneaking up on Patches," she said.

Sam nodded in agreement.

"But who do you like the best? Elmo or Patches?" Becca asked.

A slight movement from Sam told Jesse that his son had pointed at his preference.

"*Ach*, pointing at the picture will never do. Can you say his name out loud for me?" Becca asked, her voice calm and inviting.

There was a long, quiet pause. Becca didn't intrude. She gave Sam plenty of time to think. And then, the softest whisper wafted across the room. So quiet that Jesse almost didn't hear.

"Patches."

Jesse blinked. Had he heard right? Had Sam actually said the dog's name out loud?

"That's very *gut*," Becca said. "But why do you like Patches the best?"

Every nerve in Jesse's body went on high alert. He leaned forward slightly, eager to hear his son's response. Would Sam speak again? Could he do it?

"Dog," Sam whispered low.

Okay, not a complete sentence, but Jesse understood only too well. Before Alice had died, Sam had asked him numerous times if they could get a dog. They already had several barn cats who kept the mice population down but Sam wanted a puppy of his very own. Jesse hadn't gotten around to getting the boy one before tragedy had struck and then they'd moved here to Colorado. Maybe it was time…

"Very *gut*," Becca said, closing the book with a slight snap. "You're doing so well, Sam. I'm very pleased with you."

She leaned her head down and kissed the boy's forehead. When they stood, Jesse pulled back into the kitchen with a quick jerk. He didn't want to be caught eavesdropping, yet he felt mesmerized by the two of them. He could listen to them all day.

Hurrying over to the kitchen sink, he noticed that all the dishes had been washed and put away. He stared at the clean countertops, stunned down to the tips of his worn work boots.

"We're all done for this evening." Becca spoke from behind and he turned.

She stood in the doorway, holding Sam's hand. The boy smiled shyly but didn't speak.

"How did he do tonight?" Jesse asked, clearing his throat.

"*Wundervoll*. He even spoke twice," she said.

"*Ja*, I heard. That's great news."

Jesse smiled at his son, trying not to overreact so much that it startled Sam and shut him down. Jesse had enough common sense not to push the boy until he was ready. But it was an amazing, wonderful start. And he had Becca to thank for all of it.

Chapter Six

"I see you've finished making more chairs for the table. You're a *gut* carpenter." Becca glanced around the kitchen in Jesse's home and couldn't help admiring his simple handiwork.

There were now four wooden chairs surrounding the long table, which had enough room to seat eight people. That wasn't surprising. Most Amish families had an average of seven or eight children. But since Jesse's wife had died, Becca wondered why he had made such a large table. Maybe he hoped to remarry and have more children. She wasn't sure. She figured he'd lost all his furniture in the house fire and it would take time to rebuild. Already, she'd seen enough of his house to know the walls needed painting and the cold wooden floors needed covering.

"Ahem, supper is ready. Would you like to join us in our meal?" Jesse asked.

His voice sounded a bit stilted, as though he wasn't used to having a woman in his home who wasn't his wife.

"I would like that very much."

She rolled up her sleeves and reached inside the cupboard for some plates so she could set the table. As she did so, she thought it odd that she already knew where he kept the utensils. Having washed his dishes, she knew quite a bit about his kitchen, including the fact that his cupboards were now filled with a variety of canned goods.

"I see you've got plenty of food in the house." Wearing two mitts on her hands, she lifted the casserole out of the oven and set it in the middle of the table. Steam rose from the hot dish and filled the air with a yummy aroma.

He chuckled as he sliced the loaf of homemade bread. "*Ja*, I don't want Sam to go without his meals just because I can't cook."

They sat together at the table and bowed their heads. No one spoke and Becca simply recited the Lord's Prayer in her mind. She also asked *Gott* to help Sam continue to make progress in his speaking and to help Jesse be safe while he worked on his farm.

After a few moments, Jesse released a low sigh and they dug into the delicious food. Sam ate ravenously and Becca realized it had been a long time since he and his father had enjoyed a home-cooked meal that wasn't burnt. Maybe she could do something about that from time to time, just until Jesse got back on his feet with his farm chores.

"What was the name again of the little dog in the story Becca was reading to you?" Jesse asked.

He was looking at Sam expectantly. Obviously,

he hoped the boy would respond. But he didn't. Sam glanced hesitantly at his father, then stared down at his plate. He didn't say a single word but set his fork on his plate, as though he'd lost his appetite.

The silence continued and Becca realized the mute boy had returned. To break the stilted moment, she reached across the table and squeezed Sam's chilled hand.

"It's all right," she said. Then, she looked at Jesse. "The dog's name was Patches. We had fun reading about him and Elmo."

Jesse's gaze met hers and she could see the disappointment in his eyes. Sam had spoken for her but not for his father. And that must sting Jesse pretty hard.

They finished their meal in silence and Becca quickly washed the remaining dishes. She was startled when both Sam and Jesse helped her clear the meal away.

"It's getting late. You go on up and get ready for bed. I'll be up soon to read you a story," Jesse told his son.

A glint of eagerness sparked in Sam's eyes but he merely nodded and did as asked. When they were alone, Jesse reached for a clean dish towel and started drying the dishes.

"You're *gut* with him," Jesse said.

Becca sank her hands deep into the hot, sudsy water as she scrubbed a particularly stubborn fork. "It's easy to be helpful with Sam. He's such a sweet, innocent little boy."

"I… I want to thank you for what you did tonight. I know it wasn't much and he didn't speak during dinner but just hearing his voice again was amazing," Jesse said.

She nodded. "I know. I couldn't believe it when he actually spoke. In all honesty, I didn't expect him to do it so soon and it was all I could do not to jump up and yell. It took everything in me to remain calm and act natural."

"Me too. He's comfortable around you. It's obvious you don't make him nervous." Jesse didn't look at her as he dried a spoon and placed it in a drawer.

"*Ja*, I think you're right. And that's a *gut* thing," she agreed.

"But I do. I make him too nervous to talk."

Jesse stood perfectly still. He lifted his head and looked at her, his eyes filled with a bit of misery. Becca didn't know what to say. She realized in that moment just how far apart Jesse and Sam really were. And the fact that Jesse knew it too made her feel a great deal of compassion for him. The house fire had taken more than just his wife and two daughters. In a way, it had stolen Sam from him too.

"I'm sorry, Jesse. I… I didn't mean to do anything wrong or create a problem for you," she said.

He shook his head. "*Ne*, it isn't your fault, Becca. It's mine."

She went very still as he told her about the night he'd come home to find his house on fire. Sam had cried and kept telling him it was his fault.

"The day I buried my wife and *dechder*, I was filled with such grief." He spoke in an aching whisper that caused goose bumps to cover her arms and neck. "I pushed Sam away. He tried to comfort me and I couldn't stand to even look at him. I think he knew what I was feeling inside. He'd started the fire and I blamed him for killing my *familye*. Now, he suffers from nightmares. He doesn't say anything but I know he relives the trauma of that night over and over again. We both do."

Jesse braced his hands on the countertop and hung his head. Before she could stop herself, she reached out and touched his arm.

"I'm so sorry for your loss, Jesse. So deeply sorry," she said.

He lifted his head and she saw the anguish and sorrow in his dark eyes. For just a moment, he looked bereft. She'd seen that same look in Jakob's eyes when she'd attended the funeral of his first wife after she'd died in childbirth. Nothing Becca could do or say could console him.

"That's why he was late for school this morning. He'd had a bad nightmare and it took a long time for me to calm him down," Jesse said.

Ah, so now she knew. He hadn't been cruel to the boy. Sam had simply had a nightmare and been crying. Jesse had tried to comfort the boy. He wasn't an abusive father. Not from what she could see. He was just a grieving father and husband who was trying to help his troubled son. And knowing this brought Becca a great deal of respect for Jesse as well as a ton of relief. The fact that he had confided in her softened her heart.

Jesse swallowed hard and took a deep breath before glancing out the window. "It's dark already and you should be home where you'll be safe. It's time for you to go."

He didn't wait for her approval before he reached for her heavy, black shawl, scarf and warm traveling bonnet and handed them to her. He watched her silently as she put them on. Then, he walked her outside where he harnessed her horse to her buggy.

"I can see the lights of your farm late at night," he said.

"*Ja*, Jakob will leave a kerosene lamp burning for me until I arrive home safely. If it gets too late, he'll *komm* looking for me."

"I figured as much. The roads are very icy. I'll watch for the light. If it stays on, I'll know you're in trouble and will *komm* find you. If the light goes out, I'll know you've arrived home safe."

Since they didn't have cell phones, this system would work. She let him take her hand as he helped her climb into her buggy. "I'll turn off the light as soon as I arrive home."

He nodded and, taking the leather lead lines into her gloved hands, she slapped them lightly on her horse's rump. Even though it was only eight o'clock, it had been a long day and she was eager to get home. Because they got up at four in the morning, most Amish were in bed by this time. Perhaps she had stayed too long. She still had lesson plans to review for tomorrow. She would take the kerosene light to her room on the opposite side of her house, so Jesse wouldn't be able to see it from his farm and get worried about her. No doubt she'd be up late preparing for school in the morning.

Within minutes, her horse had pulled onto the main county road. In the moonlight, she could see the shimmer of black ice on the asphalt. She drove very slowly and, as her horse settled into an even rhythm, she hoped they wouldn't encounter any automotive vehicles before she reached the turnoff to her cousin's farm. It was dangerous to drive a horse and buggy in the dark.

She stayed stiff and alert and, when she reached her home safely, she breathed a sigh of relief. Almost everyone in the house was already in bed but Aunt Naomi greeted her wearing her warm flannel nightgown and carrying a bright kerosene lamp.

"I was getting worried about you," the woman said, peering at Becca to ensure she was all right.

"There was no need." Becca spoke softly so she wouldn't awaken the others. "I did some *gut* work with little Sam this night. He spoke for the first time, *Aent* Naomi. It was only a whisper, but he spoke twice."

"*Ach*, that's *wundervoll*. I'm so glad. Now, let's go to bed. Tomorrow will come soon enough."

"You go on. I'll be up in just a few minutes," Becca said.

Satisfied that her niece was home safe, Naomi handed her the kerosene lamp before disappearing up the dark stairs.

Becca carried the lamp over to the kitchen window facing Jesse's hay field. She turned the light up bright, hoping he would see it. Then, she turned it off, knowing he would get the message that she was home safe.

Moving silently through the darkness, she entered her bedroom and pulled a chair over to the window. She rested her cheek against the cool windowsill, thinking perhaps she could delay her schoolwork for one more day. Because honestly, she was too tired to do any more tonight.

Lying on the bed, she closed her eyes and tried to rest. But her mind was too active to sleep. She thought about all that had happened that evening. Sam had spoken and Jesse had revealed some deeply personal things to her. She knew without a doubt that he was still powerfully in love with his deceased wife. He was still grieving for her and their two daughters. And perhaps that was for the best. She was Sam's teacher and had helped him make substantial progress today. That was her job. It was the career she had chosen for herself. She didn't need anything else. So, why couldn't she stop wishing for more?

Jesse stood on his back porch and gazed into the dark. Far across the rocky fields, a small pinpoint of light could be seen, coming from the Fishers' farmhouse. No more than a faint glow that flickered among the dark, barren trees bordering their two property lines. And yet, it was so clear. Like a beacon lighting the way for a ship lost at sea. Just a pale glow but easy enough to see. Jesse knew it was way past the time when Becca and her *familye* should have gone to bed. And because the light persisted, he started to worry about her. What if her horse and buggy had gone off the frozen road? What if she was stranded in a snowbank and needed his help? Maybe she hadn't made it home yet. Maybe she was hurt.

He turned, prepared to wake up Sam so he could go looking for Becca. But the light went out abruptly and he released a pensive exhale. She was home safe. He knew her cousins wouldn't turn out the light until she was there. Jesse could finally go to bed and rest, though he knew he would find very little sleep. His mind was too filled with riotous thoughts. Memories of his past happiness and the burden of guilt for losing it all.

Entering his kitchen, he was careful not to let the screen door clap closed and wake up Sam. He doffed his boots, making his way through the dark house in his stockinged feet. He had a hole in the big toe of his right sock but didn't plan to darn it, or any of his other socks and shirts, anytime soon. Sewing had been Alice's task and he doubted he could do a decent job of it. Maybe he could hire one of the Amish women from church to do his mending. Until then, he'd just put up with the holes.

After building up the kindling in the potbellied stove, he walked up the creaking stairs and paused just before Sam's doorway to listen. No restless shifting or low cries came from the room. His son was fast asleep, seeming content for the night. And Jesse knew they had Becca to thank for that.

Grateful for all that had transpired this evening, he made his way to his own room where he sat on the mattress and removed his woolen socks. As he lay back on the cool covers, his mind was filled with wonder. *Gott* had truly blessed them this night. Sam had finally spoken for the first time in over a year. It wasn't much, just two little words that were said in a quiet whisper. But it was enough. Sam had talked. Finally.

Until they got to the dinner table.

Then, the child had looked at Jesse and clammed up tight as a fist. Jesse knew it was because Sam feared him. Because the boy felt guilty for what he had done. And yet, there was no anger in Jesse toward his son. No guile or recriminations. Not anymore. The boy was only a young child. What had happened hadn't been his fault. Not really. Jesse was the patriarch of his home. If the house fire had been anyone's fault, it was his.

He wanted Sam to be happy. To go on and live a joyful life filled with good works. When Jesse had watched Becca's buggy pull away from his home, he'd been touched by her kindness. She'd provided them with a tasty supper. She'd washed the dishes and brought order to his house. And laughter. For just a moment, he had wished she could stay. But she wasn't Alice. She wasn't his wife. And he felt disloyal for being drawn in by her winsome smiles and easy manner as she moved around his home.

After she'd left, he'd kept his word and read a bedtime story to Sam. It had been a surprisingly pleasant task. Jesse had read one of the books Becca had brought them. Acting out the voices of each character, he'd made Sam smile several times. He'd even tried Becca's tactic and asked the boy who was his favorite person in the story. But Sam hadn't said a word. He'd simply pointed at the mother in the story and Jesse's heart had filled with so much pain that he thought he'd cry right then and there in front of his son.

Sam missed Alice. So did Jesse. More than he could say. He loved her with all his heart, mind and strength. And he could not forget her. No, not ever.

Sam's words spoken to Becca that evening hadn't been much but, in his heart of hearts, Jesse had cheered loud and hard the moment he'd heard them. Finally. Finally, Sam had spoken again. And if he could do it twice, he could do it again. Surely the dam of silence had been broken open. The boy obviously felt comfortable and safe with Becca. But that didn't matter to Jesse. Because other than educating Sam, Jesse must not let the pretty schoolteacher impact his emotions or his life any more than that. No, sirree. Not one single bit.

Chapter Seven

By Saturday morning, the skies had cleared to an azure blue. Rainstorms had all but dissipated the snow across the countryside, leaving the earth saturated and smelling of musty, damp soil. As Becca drove the horse and buggy over to Jesse's farm, she didn't care a bit. It was still early and, though she was glad the day was clear and free of wind for this outing, she was too happy and excited to worry about the weather.

Aunt Naomi and her eight-year-old granddaughter, Ruby, sat beside Becca on the seat. On her lap, Naomi held her sixteen-month-old granddaughter, Chrissie. Jakob, his wife, Abby, and *Dawdi* Zeke rode in a horse-drawn wagon behind them, with ten-year-old Reuben in the back. A sense of exhilaration swarmed Becca's chest when she considered the surprise they were about to offer Jesse and Sam. The buggy and wagon were laden with a nice lunch, hand tools, buckets of off-white paint and brushes, three large rag rugs that Aunt Naomi didn't need anymore, and plain muslin cloth to make curtains for Jesse's windows.

Dressed in a black chambray shirt, Jesse was just crossing from the barn to his house when they pulled into his graveled driveway. When he saw the long entourage, he stopped and stared with wide eyes and a crinkled forehead. At the noisy rattle of the harness and wagon, Sam came running from the chicken coop. Becca was startled to see a little black-and-white puppy bounding at the boy's heels. Like his father, Sam gaped in surprise at the buggy and wagon. But when he saw Becca, he grinned and ran straight toward her.

"Guder mariye." Dawdi Zeke waved a wrinkled hand in the air. Jakob hopped down off the wagon first, then reached up a supporting arm to help his wife and the elderly man down off the high seat.

"Guder daag," Jesse greeted them, a heavy dose of curiosity filling his eyes.

Becca had stepped out of the buggy and greeted Sam.

"Hallo! Do you have a new puppy?" she asked, eyeing the little furball who gave several shrill barks.

Sam nodded and picked up the mutt, snuggling it close beneath his chin.

"What have you named it?" she asked.

Sam looked down and scuffed his booted feet against the damp gravel. He glanced nervously at Naomi, who still sat in the buggy.

"Patches." Jesse spoke nearby, looking a bit embarrassed. "I suggested he name the dog after the story in his book, and he acknowledged that he liked that."

Becca smiled up at him. "*Ach*, so you got him a dog. I'm glad. I'm sure that pleased Sam."

It was a statement, not a question. And she couldn't have been happier. This gesture more than anything showed her what a kind, loving father Jesse really was inside. He'd been hurt and seemed all gruff and disapproving but Becca was quickly learning otherwise.

She reached into the buggy to take the baby while Aunt Naomi and Ruby hopped down. As the men spoke together, her ears were tuned to every bit of conversation going on around her. A feeling of happiness hummed inside of her. Last night at supper, Aunt Naomi had suggested they have a work project today, to help Jesse and his son. And the entire *familye* had agreed it would be fun, as well as beneficial to the King *familye*. Becca had concurred.

When she turned around, she caught Jesse staring at her. Something in his eyes told her he was both irritated and glad to see them here. His gaze swept over her, taking in the domestic scene as she cuddled Chrissie close in her arms. Suddenly, Becca felt out of sorts and a rush of heat stained her face. She hoped he didn't think this was her idea and she was being forward. Though she'd been over to his farm three times this past week to tutor Sam, she didn't want Jesse to believe she was interested in him romantically. Because she wasn't. No, absolutely not.

Deciding to let the men take the lead, she bounced the baby on her hip and waited.

"What brings you here to my place so early on a Saturday morning?" Jesse asked Jakob and *Dawdi* Zeke.

Jakob stepped forward to explain, his smile wide, his tone filled with a pleasantness that none of them could deny. "You've been a member of our *Gmay* for over three months now. Though you've never asked any of us for help, we understand you need some repairs done around your place. We know you can do the work over time, but it's winter now and some of the chores should be done immediately. If you'll allow us to assist you, the women will paint the inside of your house while us men repair your leaky roof and broken fence posts. Then you'll be ready to buy the livestock you need. And later, the women have prepared a nice lunch for us all to enjoy. We're here at your disposal, so use us well."

Jesse frowned and Becca held her breath. He hesitated, looking at all of them. They waited. No one said a word. But it was obvious they were hoping he would agree. Finally, it was *Dawdi* Zeke who broke the silence.

"*Ach*, of course he'll use us. We're here to work and that's what we'll do." The elderly man hobbled over to the back of the wagon and lifted out a silver toolbox. Without waiting for an invitation, he shambled toward the house.

"Where's your ladder?" he called over his shoulder in a commanding voice.

That spurred everyone into action. The men and Reuben hurried after him while the women gathered up their paintbrushes. Sam stayed close beside

Becca. He clicked his fingers and the puppy scampered after him. She was surprised to see that he'd trained the dog to follow him with just a snap of his fingers.

"Jakob, don't let your *dawdi* up on that roof," Aunt Naomi called to her son.

At the age of ninety-six, *Dawdi* Zeke was too old and frail to be climbing any ladders. Naomi looked so concerned that Jakob tugged on his grandfather's arm.

"*Dawdi*, I don't want you up on that roof. *Mamm* would skin me alive if you fell and got hurt," Jakob said.

Zeke simply laughed. "*Ach*, of course I'm not going up, though I've been on more roofs than you can shake a stick at. But those days are long gone now. I'll stay safely on the ground and hand you up the wood and shingles you'll need."

"*Gut*. That will really help us out. Then we won't have to climb down as often and you can supervise things on the ground," Jesse said.

He sounded so positive that Becca wondered if he'd just needed friendship to open him up to the man he really was inside…to smile and be happy again. Either way, it was quite nice of Jesse to look out for her grandfather. It told her that he was considerate and respectful of the old man.

Dawdi Zeke clapped a hand on Jesse's shoulder and nodded with approval. His gray eyes danced with a zest for life and that's when Jesse smiled wide. It was infectious. Everyone felt happy today. Becca knew work frolics were like that. They were always a lot of fun. An opportunity to serve others and accomplish some worthwhile tasks for someone else. Knowing they could visit while they worked and that a nice meal awaited them was all the reward they needed.

"*Komm* on, let's get to work," Naomi called to the women and girls.

Carrying the baby and a bucket of paint, Becca followed them inside the house. Sam scurried after her, the puppy clambering at his heels. The boy didn't speak but he held up a forbidding hand and made Patches stay outside. Becca could see why. The dog's paws were muddy and would dirty the floors. She was delighted to see that Sam had a new friend and was actively training the little pup.

Becca almost told Sam to join the men. After all, he should learn from the hands of his father what he should do. But then she thought better of it. Maybe the boy needed a little more time to grow more confident. Later, once he was speaking regularly again, then he could join Jesse and the other men.

Since she'd been here before, Becca showed Naomi and Abby what needed to be done. Ruby was given the chore of tending the baby and fetching things for them now and then. With her arms free, Becca was able to set to work, helping to clean the house thoroughly from stem to stern. Sam helped all he could, scrubbing, fetching and carrying.

The women painted the living room first, the kitchen second and then the bathroom. As they finished removing the plastic drop cloths from the wooden floors, Becca and Abby carried in the large rag rugs with Sam's help. The heavy braids weaved together were big but looked absolutely lovely in the middle of the living room floor. Becca admired the colorful pattern for just a moment, thinking how pleased Jesse would be to have something warm beneath his bare feet. Then, she turned away. *Hochmut* was the pride of the world and something the Amish shunned. She must not allow herself to dwell on such things.

Their afternoon work would see them finish painting the three bedrooms upstairs, while Naomi measured and hand-stitched some modest curtains for the bare windows.

Now, it was time for lunch. Becca's stomach growled loudly as she wondered how the morning had passed so quickly. She stepped into the kitchen to lay out their noon meal, still able to hear the other women's jolly voices coming from the living room.

"Many hands make light work," Aunt Naomi answered her unasked question. "Look at what we've accomplished already. Jesse and Sam will be much more comfortable in their house after this. Those poor dears. I can't imagine how awful it's been, living here without Sam's *mudder* to love and care for them. A home needs a woman's touch, and that's all. Too bad our Becca isn't interested in marrying the man."

From the open doorway, Becca saw Abby surveying the empty living room as she sat in a rocking chair with Chrissie. "*Ach*, it's still a very empty house but at least it's clean now. And Becca could have any man she wanted. She'd make a real catch for some *gut* Amish man."

"*Ja*, she would. The house is definitely much more cheerful now. Those filthy walls made me want to shudder. And it was time for Jesse to make friends. We're his neighbors and his brothers and sisters in the faith. It's time for him to be a part of our *Gmay*," Naomi said.

As she lifted the heavy basket that contained their lunch onto the table, Becca silently agreed. Friendship would go a long way to healing Jesse and Sam's broken hearts. As the boy's teacher, this was all Becca could offer and she hoped it helped.

She laid a fresh loaf of bread on the pristine counter, wondering if the men had made as much progress with their chores. She glanced up at the windowsill, analyzing her paint job with a critical eye.

Oh, no! She'd missed a spot. Not very much but it was noticeable if you looked up. She'd just fix it before she finalized lunch preparations. It wouldn't take more than a moment to run the paintbrush over the narrow area and no one would even know it was there.

Pulling the ladder over to the sink, she climbed up. Dipping her brush into a bucket, she concentrated on her task as the ladder wobbled slightly. She quickly ran the bristles over the trim surrounding the windowsill, then set the brush across the lip of the bucket. There! It was almost perfect.

She was just climbing down when she lost her footing. A moment of panic rushed up her throat and she clawed the air for something, anything to hold onto. It did no good and she felt herself falling!

"Ooff!" Jesse's breath left him in a sudden exhale as he caught Becca before she could fall off the ladder.

She clasped his neck with one arm, the side of her face smooshed beneath his chin. He held her there for several long seconds, giving her a moment to recover her footing. Her sweet, clean fragrance spiraled around him as she stepped on his toes. Thankfully he was wearing heavy boots.

"*Ach*, I'm so sorry!" she exclaimed, pulling back just a bit.

He still had his arms wrapped around her tiny waist. Looking down, he locked his gaze with hers. Her face was so close to his that he could feel her warm breath against his cheek. He saw the confusion in her startled blue eyes. Her pink lips rounded in a circle of surprise. He could feel her soft fingertips against the back of his neck.

"*Geht es dir gut?*" he asked, his voice low and soft.

"*Ja, ja*! I'm all right," she said rather breathlessly.

"Ahem!"

Someone cleared their throat and he looked up and saw Naomi and Abby standing in the doorway.

Becca quickly pulled free and moved over to the stove. She patted her *kapp*, thrusting stray curls of golden hair back into the head covering. She looked as flustered as he felt.

"*Danke* for catching me." She spoke without looking at him.

"Did you fall?" Naomi asked.

"*Ja*, I fell off the ladder," Becca quickly explained, seeming embarrassed that the women might think she'd done something inappropriate.

"*Ach*, it's a *gut* thing that Jesse was here to catch you." Abby spoke with a knowing smile.

Naomi walked to the sink where she began washing red apples. "*Ja*, it was a very *gut* thing."

If Jesse didn't know better, he would think the older woman's voice sounded a bit strangled, as if she were trying not to laugh.

Having recovered her composure, Becca busied herself with setting the long table. He was suddenly highly aware of her as a lovely, desirable woman. And that thought left him feeling nervous and out of sorts.

"Um, I'll tell the men we're just about ready to eat," he said, practically bounding out the back door.

Anything to escape. He had to get out of this room right now. Had to get away from Becca and her innocent, confused looks and her aunt's knowing glances.

"*Komm* eat," he called to the other men.

He waited for them to climb down off the roof before following them into the house. No way was he going to be alone with these women again. He needed the other men as a buffer zone.

After prayer, the men sat at the table while the women hovered around seeing that their plates were filled. Abby spread a blanket on the floor in the living room for the children to sit and enjoy a little picnic of sorts. Jesse regretted that he had only four chairs made. With just himself and Sam living in the house, he thought there was no need to make any more. But now, he realized he needed double the number of seats if he was to accommodate his new friends. And the thought of making more chairs made him feel happy inside. It gave him a purpose. Something to work toward.

"How is the work going on the roof?" Naomi asked as she laid another piece of fried chicken on Jakob's plate.

"*Gut*! We've finished the roof and it should weather any future storms," he replied.

"*Ja*, we should have plenty of time this afternoon to work on the barn and broken fence posts before it's time to leave." *Dawdi* Zeke popped an entire boiled egg into his mouth and chewed with relish.

"And you *weibsleit*? How has your work gone?" Jakob asked. He glanced around the room, seeing the fresh coat of paint on the walls.

"We have finished downstairs. This afternoon, we'll finish painting the bedrooms," Naomi said.

The group chatted about their work and inconsequential things. Jakob offered to sell one of his best milk cows to Jesse and discussed the Rocky Mountain Expo Select Sale to be held at the National Western Complex in Denver next month.

"Bishop Yoder and Harley Troyer are the auctioneers. You can get all the draft horses and mules you need," *Dawdi* Zeke said.

"*Ja*, and in April, they'll hold a draft horse and equipment auction in Brighton. Us men commission a small bus from town and hire an *Englischer* to drive us there. They've gotten to know us Amish and will haul the livestock here to Riverton in a trailer. You're *willkomm* to go with us and see if there's something worth buying for your farm," Jakob said.

Jesse nodded. This was just the info he needed to acquire some good livestock to work his place. He glanced at Sam, wondering what to do with the boy while he was gone.

"I'll watch him for you," Becca said.

He glanced up at her as she leaned over his shoulder to refill his glass with chilled milk from the well house. Funny how she always seemed to anticipate his needs and offer to help even before he asked. Though Jesse hadn't asked, he was grateful for all that Becca and her *familye* had done. For the first time in months, he felt like he had real friends. People he could count on for help.

"*Danke*, that would be great," he said, conscious of Naomi watching him with glowing eyes.

Oh, no! He knew that look. The look of an Amish mother who wanted to make a match for her daughter. Except that Becca was Naomi's niece.

Same difference.

He looked away, feeling like a silly schoolboy who was smitten by his first girl. And he wasn't. Smitten, that is. Not with Becca. No, sirree. Nor was he a silly schoolboy. He was a fully-grown married man and the father of three. Or at least he used to be. Now, he wasn't grounded anymore. He couldn't get a feel for who he was and what he should be doing. It was as if the pieces no longer fit together. Somehow, he'd lost his way. He'd been clinging to his faith, hoping he found his path through the darkness.

They finished their meal and everyone returned to their tasks. Jesse was grateful to be back at his labors. Work was something he understood. A distraction that made him forget the pain. For a few short hours, he could pretend that everything was just fine. That Alice and the kids were back at the house and he'd see them all later that evening when he came in for supper. That he'd laugh, tickle and play with them like he used to do.

It was several hours later when Jesse returned to the house for some plastic cups and a jug of water. The men were thirsty and, as their host, he had hurried to accommodate them. He planned to slip in and out of the kitchen without being noticed. But Becca was there, sitting in a hardbacked chair as she fed baby Chrissie.

"Hallo." She greeted him with a soft smile.

He nodded, going directly to the cupboard where he knew the cups were kept. As he pulled the door open, he couldn't help noticing the tidiness of the room, not a dirty dish in sight. The air smelled of fresh paint and he caught a yummy whiff of something good cooking in the oven. When he glanced in that direction, Becca offered an explanation.

"It's your supper. We thought you might appreciate something to eat this evening after all of us have left," she said.

"You didn't need to do that. I've got lots of canned goods in the house and have gotten quite good at heating up soup for Sam's dinner."

"It was no trouble." She lifted a spoon to the baby's mouth. Like a little bird, Chrissie opened wide.

It seemed his guests had thought of everything, taking care of him and Sam like they would their own *familye*. He shouldn't be surprised. It was the Amish way. Alice had done the same on numerous occasions, taking meals in to another *familye*, tending their sick children, washing their dirty laundry, doing whatever she could to ease their load. And it made him love her and his faith even more. He cherished the way they looked after one another. If only Alice and the girls were still here, he could feel whole again. That was why he'd left Pennsylvania. To hide from the memories. But they'd followed him here. And he knew he had to figure out how to go on without them.

As he filled the jug with water from the kitchen tap, he glanced over at Becca. She'd propped little Chrissie on the table and had wrapped a dish towel around her neck so she wouldn't soil her dress as she ate. Keeping one hand on the child's leg so she wouldn't fall off the table, Becca spooned in something that looked like mashed potatoes.

"You seem so natural with *kinder*," he said.

Becca gave a sad little laugh. "I hope so, since I teach an entire school full of them. But you wouldn't have thought so during my first week here."

He chuckled, remembering how flustered she was that day he'd walked in on her class when it erupted into absolute chaos. "Everyone is bound to have a bad day now and then. Have you had any more snake incidents?"

She laughed. "*Ne*, thankfully."

He shut off the faucet and reached for the lid to the jug. As he screwed it on with several quick twists of his wrist, he asked a question that had been on his mind for quite some time.

"Instead of teaching, I would have thought you would be married by now and have *kinder* of your own."

She didn't respond right off and he looked at her. Her eyebrows were creased with consternation and a flash of pain filled her eyes.

"*Ach*, I always wanted to marry and have *kinder* of my own but it didn't work out. I… I was engaged once," she said.

Oh. Maybe he shouldn't have asked. He instantly regretted his question. It was too private. Too personal.

"I'm sorry. I didn't mean to pry," he said, feeling like a heel.

She shook her head and fed the baby another bite of food. "*Ne*, it's all right. I'm better off, actually. I would never want to marry a man who didn't love me. And it would be even worse if he loved someone else."

Okay, his curiosity was piqued. Even though it wasn't his business, he couldn't leave without knowing more.

"What happened?" he asked.

He set the cups and water jug aside as he leaned his hip against the counter.

She shrugged and wiped a dribble of potato from the baby's chin. "Nothing, really. I'd known Vernon all my life. We went to school together and always planned to marry one day. Everyone expected it."

Jesse sensed the admission caused her some embarrassment, as if it was something to be ashamed of.

"Did you still love him?" Jesse asked.

"Perhaps. But it didn't matter. He'd discovered that he was in love with Ruth, another girl in our *Gmay*. It seemed they'd developed feelings for each other that went beyond friendship. I'd always wondered why he refused to set our wedding date. Now I know it was because he...he didn't want me anymore."

"I'm sorry," he said.

His heart ached for her. He could just imagine how it must have hurt her, living in a *Gmay* with a boy that everyone thought loved her. And then the embarrassment and pain of finding out he preferred someone else. All her broken dreams must have been painful but also demoralizing. No wonder she had wanted to leave and go somewhere else to start over again. He'd done the same thing after Alice and their girls had died.

She met his gaze, her eyes filled with strength and courage. "Don't be sorry. It was a blessing. Vernon and I would have been unhappy together. We'd been *gut* friends all our lives but we'd grown apart. He thought I read too many books and was way too opinionated and I thought he was too domineering. We wouldn't have gotten on well together. And I love teaching. I decided to make that my profession. I love working with the *kinder*. It's a *gut* career choice for an unmarried Amish girl like me. I just wish I didn't have to return to Ohio at the end of the school year. Vernon and Ruth will be married next fall and I'd really rather not be there to watch it happen."

Ah, he understood now. He could read between the lines. She didn't want to watch the man she had loved for so long marry another girl and start a *familye* together. And being Amish, that must hurt Becca even more because she was still single. In fact, Becca was quite old to be unmarried. By Amish standards, she was an old maid. But now, it appeared that she had decided she wanted to spend her life teaching. It was a noble profession too and he was glad she'd found something fulfilling and worthwhile to do.

He tilted his head to the side. "Why do you have to leave here? Why not stay?"

She shrugged before lifting Chrissie down off the table. The toddler waved her chubby arms and laughed. She was so sweet and innocent and she immediately reminded Jesse of his own two little girls.

"My teaching assignment will be finished when school lets out the first of May," Becca said. "By next fall, Caroline Schwartz will have recovered from her accident and can resume her teaching assignment. I can't live off my relatives without finding some kind of employment. And Riverton is too small a town to offer many jobs, let alone another teaching position in another Amish school. I'll have to leave to find work. The logical choice is to go home, so I have a place to live until I can find another position."

Hmm. For some odd reason, he didn't like the thought of her leaving. She'd been so good for Sam. She'd been good for him too.

"You could find a different teaching assignment here in Colorado," he suggested.

She gave a sad little laugh. "I'm afraid there aren't that many Amish settlements here, let alone vacant teaching positions for their schools. The only reason I got this assignment was because I have *familye* here and they knew me well enough to give the school board a recommendation for me."

"Perhaps you'll find another position somewhere in Ohio or Pennsylvania. Maybe you won't have to go home after all," he said.

Even as he suggested the idea, he knew it was unlikely. Unless they were in a real bind, the Amish preferred to hire someone they knew and trusted to teach their precious children. Each *Gmay* had their own *Ordnung*, the unwritten rules they followed within their unique community. Unless Becca married one of their men and agreed to abide by their *Ordnung*, she would be an outsider in another Amish community. They would never hire her to teach their kids.

"*Ach*, I better get back to work. We're almost finished painting Sam's bedroom and the *weibsleit* need my help." She stood and walked to the door.

"*Ja*, I best get back to work too."

He wished he could stay and ask her more questions about her life. He found her quite interesting and he respected her pioneering spirit and desire to have a career rather than marry. It couldn't have been easy for her to come here to a strange land to live and work. But it wouldn't be proper for him to keep talking to her right now. She was hurting, just like him. And he didn't want to remind her of that pain. Besides, the *mannsleit* were waiting for him to bring them water.

As he carried the cups and jug outside, he found it hard to believe that Vernon would cast Becca aside for someone else. Becca would make the perfect Amish wife. Besides being capable of cleaning and running a household, she was an excellent cook and was beautiful and knowledgeable. Fascinating to talk to. When he was with her, he could almost forget his broken heart.

Almost.

If the situation were different, he might be willing to ask Jakob if he could court her. But Jesse couldn't forget about Alice. His heart still ached for his sweet wife. In his mind, he was still married to her and he couldn't let her go.

He'd heard of some Amish widowers with children marrying a woman for convenience. He thought about approaching Becca and Jakob, to see if they might agree to such an arrangement. After all, he badly needed a wife and Sam needed a mother. Becca needed a permanent place to stay so she wouldn't have to return to Ohio. But no. A loveless marriage wouldn't be fair to Becca. Or him, for that matter. Both of them deserved so much more. Besides, she'd just said she wouldn't marry a man who didn't love her. And right now, he couldn't offer her what both of them really wanted and needed most of all. A home where they'd be loved and cherished. A real marriage in deed as well as in name. Even without asking Becca, he knew that neither of them would settle for anything less. Not now. Not ever. It was that simple.

Chapter Eight

On Thursday evening, another snowstorm settled across the valley and didn't move all night long. Becca awoke the following morning to find six inches of the white stuff covering the countryside. She got up early to prepare for her day, wondering if she should cancel school. After all, it would take a lot of effort for parents to drive their horses and buggies through the heavy drifts. Maybe it was best for the kids to stay home. But the bishop had told her they rarely canceled school because they had to meet the state attendance requirements each year. And the plows were good to get out early and clear the county roads.

"You sure you'll be all right driving to school alone?" Jakob asked her at the breakfast table.

She nodded, knowing he would make time to drive her if she felt uncertain about the task. "I'll be fine."

Her cousin smiled with approval. As children, he had teased her for being a tomboy. Athletic and full of life, she was always the girl who could do anything. But since those carefree days, she wasn't so sure anymore. Vernon's rejection had hit her confidence rather hard. He'd broken her heart and destroyed her trust in men.

Bundled up in her scarf, gloves and black traveling bonnet, she left early and drove extra carefully. No doubt she'd have to shovel the sidewalks at the school. She wanted time to build up a fire in the old stove so the schoolhouse was warm and toasty for the scholars when they arrived.

As she turned off onto the snowy dirt road leading to Bishop Yoder's hay fields, she saw the school. A thin stream of gray smoke rose from the chimney and she gave a cry of pleasure. Someone was already here. Probably one of the school board members, taking care of the school and seeing that they had their needs met.

As she pulled into the main yard, she saw a lone man standing beside the front porch, shoveling snow off the walk paths. Even from this distance, she recognized the solid set of his broad shoulders and the tenacious tilt of his black felt hat.

Jesse King.

And little Sam was just carrying another armful of kindling into the schoolhouse.

Tugging on the lead lines, Becca stuck her tongue in her cheek and couldn't contain a quiet laugh. It was the snowiest day of the year and Jesse had finally gotten Sam to school on time.

"Hallo!" she called, stepping out of the buggy with a flurry of lavender skirts.

Jesse paused in his work and leaned an arm against the handle of his snow shovel. He tugged the brim of his hat away from his face in a completely male stance and gazed at her with no emotion on his face whatsoever. But his dark eyes were filled with life. His breath exhaled in small puffs, his cheeks gleaming red above his beard.

"Guder mariye," he said in a low voice.

She made her way through the snow, stamping her feet when she reached the cement walk path he had unburied. "What are you doing here so early?"

He glanced at the cleared walk paths, which were quickly melting now that he'd removed the snow. "I would think that is obvious. I'm shoveling snow."

She laughed. "I know that, silly. But I didn't expect to see you here so early. *Danke* for clearing away the snow and starting the fire."

Jesse shrugged, a slight frown tugging at his forehead. "It's the least I can do to repay you for all the meals and tutoring you've been giving us. Besides, it's the duty of the fathers of the scholars to look after the school, unless they make an exception and assign these chores to someone. Bishop Yoder and the other men have more *kinder* than me, so I thought it'd be easier for me to do the task today."

How thoughtful of him. Yes, it was true that the board members were to look after the school's needs. But Becca knew each father had a farm and *familye* to care for too. Sometimes, it was easy to neglect the school just a bit. And even though she knew it was expected, she couldn't help feeling happy that Jesse had come to her aid. He'd saved her from the arduous chore of shoveling snow and fetching wood. Not that she minded the work. It was just nice to have it done already. Jesse's efforts told her that he wasn't as callous and harsh as he pretended to be. No, he was a kind and generous man and she appreciated his work on her behalf.

She scooped up a handful of snow and smashed it into a round ball between her gloved hands. "The snow is heavy. There's lots of water in it."

He grinned at that and she stared, simply because it wasn't often that she saw this man looking happy.

"*Ja*, it'll fill our rivers and streams," he said.

Feeling a bit reckless, she tossed the snowball at him, hitting him squarely in the middle of the chest. She laughed, thinking he might throw a snowball back at her but he didn't. He merely looked down at the splotch of snow marring his heavy black coat and then back at her. Without a word, he brushed the snow away.

Feeling suddenly awkward, she glanced up at the gray sky and shivered at the cold. "I may let school out early today. *Dawdi* Zeke thinks another storm is on its way. I need to give the scholars their assignments for the end-of-year program but I don't want them stranded here all night."

She mentally calculated that they had plenty of water to drink and fuel to burn but she had very little food, except for what the scholars brought in their lunch pails. If she had to feed the children before their parents could break through the snow to retrieve them the following morning, they'd be mighty hungry.

He inclined his head. "That's wise. I'll plan to pick up Sam at noon. That should give each *familye* plenty of time to return home before the next storm hits."

"But what about Sam's tutoring this afternoon?" she asked.

"*Ne*, you shouldn't *komm* over today. You go home where it's safe. It won't hurt him to miss one session."

"All right. Let's hope the next storm bypasses us altogether. I've never seen so much snow in all my life. And I'm sorry to say this but I'm rather tired of it now." She laughed, amazed at the colder weather here in Colorado.

He chuckled too and she couldn't help jerking in surprise at the sudden sound. He'd actually laughed! Maybe he hadn't been as disgusted by her throwing a snowball at him as she first thought.

"*Ja*, we definitely have lots of snow here. I had to lock Sam's dog, Patches, in the barn last night so he wouldn't wander off and get lost in the storm. Sam wanted to bring the pup inside to sleep with him but I said *ne*," he said, a wide smile curving his lips.

She stared at him in amazement, thinking how handsome he looked in that moment. "*Ach*, I knew you could do that."

He blinked, looking confused. "Do what?"

"Smile. It looks *gut* on you. You should do it more often."

He looked away, his expression dropping like stone. Oh, dear. Maybe she shouldn't have teased him. But she was starting to feel comfortable around this man. Maybe too comfortable. She was a grown woman and he was the father of one of her scholars. She shouldn't be flirting with him like a brainless schoolgirl.

"*Ja*, the snow here has been an adjustment. But we'll be glad to have the moisture this summer when we're watering our crops," he said, ignoring her comments altogether.

He glanced at her, looking suddenly anxious, as if he wanted to get away from her. And that's when she realized he could decide to be happy or sad. Yes, he'd faced something horrible in his life. But he could choose to be miserable and walk around with a glum face, or he could put it aside and smile. So could she. And it reminded her that, in spite of the hurt she'd suffered at the hands of Vernon, the Lord wanted her to go on and live her life. He wanted her to be happy. She was trying to do that, though it wasn't always easy. But she had the responsibility of teaching a school full of children. She must set a good example for them.

Filled with her thoughts, she turned and walked inside. Jesse leaned the shovel against the outer wall and followed her. She noticed he stomped off his boots and removed his hat at the door, then stepped inside. Sam was stacking the wood pan high with plenty of firewood to last throughout the day. The boy tossed a shy smile in her direction, then ducked his head. His father watched with approval as the boy did his work. Then, seeming assured that the school was in good condition for lessons, Jesse waved a hand.

"I'll be going now," he said.

"*Ja, danke* again. I really appreciate it," she called.

"You're *willkomm*," he said.

"See you later."

She walked with him to the door and peered outside at the chilly day. Gusts of wind were sweeping the snow into drifts along the road. As if on cue, two black buggies and horses appeared at the top of the county road. They turned off, heading toward the school. She'd kept her warm woolen shawl on so she could greet each parent, to let them know school would let out early today.

As she went out to meet them, she watched Jesse climb into his buggy and slap the leather leads gently against the horse's back. The animal lurched forward and the man waved a hand to the other families as he passed.

Thankfully, she wasn't tutoring Sam this evening. She didn't mind, not at all. But she was getting to bed rather late each night. She was tired and falling behind on her lesson plans. But Sam was speaking regularly for her now. Just simple words spoken in a mega-soft whisper within the walls of his own home, but he did talk. And she knew deep in her heart that he was making headway.

If she wasn't mistaken, so was Jesse. She sensed he wasn't an overly gregarious man by nature but he was much friendlier now, with her and her *familye* members, as well as with other people in their *Gmay*. She'd noticed him at church meetings, talking more openly with the other men, though he rarely laughed and was still shy around the women. The transition was gradual but an amazing sight to behold and she was happy for it. Now, if she could just get Sam to start speaking at school, she would consider this year a great success.

* * *

Jesse clicked his tongue, urging his horse up a particularly slippery slope as his buggy reached the county road. He thought about Becca throwing a snowball at him. No one had ever called him silly and it had been a long time since he'd felt like smiling. But lately, the urge to laugh was coming a bit easier to him. When he was with Becca, he could almost forget the sadness in his heart. Almost.

Shaking his head, he mentally reminded himself that he had to pick up Sam early today. He mustn't be late or it could put Becca in jeopardy. He knew she couldn't leave the school until all the children were gone and he didn't want to make her late getting home that afternoon. Even the slightest delay could force her to be caught in the coming snowstorm.

Looking down at the front of his coat, he saw beads of water from where her snowball had struck him. He brushed them away, feeling confused by her actions. The last girl who had flirted with him had been his wife. And yet, he didn't think that was what Becca was doing. She was just having fun. She was so full of life. He'd noticed the bounce in her step and happy lilt in her voice whenever she came over to his house. She'd confided that she'd been engaged to be married and he would have been a fool not to notice the pain in her voice. She'd been deeply hurt. All her hopes and dreams for a *familye* of her own had been dashed to pieces. It was easy to think that she'd find someone else to marry one day. That she'd go on and be just fine. But once you were really and truly in love with someone, it wasn't always that easy to move on. He knew that firsthand. Besides, she'd said she had chosen a teaching career instead of a *familye*.

When he'd been inside the school, he'd noticed how tidy everything was. Becca had made the same difference in his own home, washing the dishes when she came to tutor Sam. It had spurred him to be a better housekeeper, so he didn't appear to be taking advantage of her generosity.

Most days, she brought them something for supper too. She always claimed her aunt Naomi had made the food but he suspected she had helped. And her generosity had touched his heart. He'd heard his son's whispered words as she worked with the boy in the living room. He'd noticed how Sam's countenance lit up when he knew Becca was coming over. And honestly, Jesse had to admit he liked her frequent visits. She was working hard and making a real difference in his son's life.

As he reached the turnoff to his farm, he glanced over and saw the log house that belonged to Becca's cousin, Jakob Fisher. So different from the sprawling, white frame houses he had lived in back in Pennsylvania.

Turning toward home, he thought maybe he should speak to Bishop Yoder about Becca. He should tell him and the other board members what a good job she was doing as their schoolteacher. Then, the board would give her a good reference when it came time for her to leave and find another teaching assignment at the end of the school year. He wanted Becca to find a permanent job that would make her happy. One that would provide her with a firm and stable income all her life.

As he pulled into his main yard and directed the horse toward the barn, he felt suddenly quite sad. While he knew that Becca had to leave in the spring, he didn't want her to go. And yet, there was nothing he could do to help her stay. Nothing at all.

Chapter Nine

Jesse stepped out of the barn and glanced over at the house. After two weeks of cold, the weather had shifted. The warmth of the sun had finally melted all the snow, though the ground was quite damp. Patches romped around close by his feet, which was odd. The dog usually followed Sam everywhere. Speaking of which, where was Sam? It was Saturday morning and the boy should be outside doing his morning tasks.

Jesse had just finished his chores and was ready to head out to the fields. When he saw the two buckets of pig slop still sitting where he'd left them on the back porch almost an hour earlier, he shook his head. Why hadn't Sam fed the pigs yet?

Heaving a sigh of exasperation, he walked over to the porch and retrieved the buckets before carrying them to the pigpen. The three swine saw him coming and rushed toward him. Patches gave several shrill barks as Jesse dumped the contents of the buckets into the trough. The pigs snorted and grunted, scarfing down the food like they were starving. They were definitely overdue for their breakfast.

While the pigs were occupied, Jesse stepped inside their pen and checked their water cistern. Patches whined and scratched at the gate, trying to follow him. But no way would Jesse let the little dog in with the ornery pigs.

The temperatures were still mighty cold. Although the sky was filled with leaden clouds, he didn't think it would snow again. But it sure might rain.

Hurrying so he could get some work done in the fields before the weather turned, he used a metal bar to break the thin layer of ice that had formed over top of the water trough so the animals could drink. As he set the bar aside, he glanced toward the chicken coop, wondering if Sam had fed the hens and finished gathering the eggs yet. Stepping outside of the pigpen, he pulled the gate closed until he heard it latch, then walked toward the house with Patches at his heels. It was Saturday and they weren't in a rush to get Sam to school but Jesse needed to get out to that field if he hoped to make any progress in clearing the overgrown brush before it rained. The previous owner of this farm had gotten old and had neglected the fields, which were now overgrown by weeds, shrubs and saplings. Spring was just around the corner and Jesse wanted to make the best use of his land.

"Sam! *Waar ben jij?*" he called to his son.

He gazed at the chicken coop, expecting the boy to come from there. When he heard the screen door clap closed behind him, he whirled around and found his son standing just in front of the back door to the house. Patches scampered toward the boy, jumping at his legs. Though Sam was fully dressed for the day, his feet were bare. The boy didn't speak as Jesse walked toward him.

"What are you doing inside the house? Are you ill?" Jesse asked, feeling confused.

The boy shook his head and that's when Jesse noticed he held a book in one hand. A bad feeling settled in Jesse's stomach. Without asking, he knew what had happened. Instead of doing his farm chores, Sam had been inside the house reading.

"Did you feed the chickens and gather the eggs yet? Did you feed the cows?" Jesse asked, hoping his son said *yes*. If so, all would be forgiven.

Sam's eyes widened and he hung his head in shame. Finally, the boy shook his head.

Jesse reached to take the book out of Sam's hand. It was a library book that Becca had given him. "You've been reading when there are chores to be done?"

Grave disappointment filled Jesse's chest. Sam hadn't done his morning chores. Not a single one. Instead, he'd been languishing inside the house. He hadn't even put on his shoes yet! As a parent, Jesse was outraged by his child's disobedience. Though he longed for a quiet heart and wanted to retain his composure, he knew he must be strict and clear in his expectations.

"Why have you not done your work yet?" Jesse asked, forcing himself to speak calmly.

Sam didn't answer but he shivered as a brisk wind

blew from the east. The child stared at his bare toes, which were scrunched against the cold, wooden porch. Jesse knew his son loved to read more than anything else. But too much of anything was not good. And Sam had plenty of time to read. In addition to school and trips to the town library every two weeks, Jesse had been reading to the boy each night, regular as clockwork. Also, for the past two months, Becca had been coming here several afternoons each week to read and tutor the boy. The strategies seemed to work. Sam's demeanor was happier and there was a bounce in the boy's step that hadn't been there for a very long time. But now, the books were getting in the way of Sam's chores. And work must always come first on a farm. It was critical to their survival. As Sam's father, Jesse had an obligation to teach his son how to work hard. To teach the boy how to farm and raise livestock. Jesse couldn't just let this go.

"I'm very disappointed in you, *sohn*. You know what is expected of you. Did you start reading and lose track of time?" Jesse asked his son.

Sam nodded.

A wave of annoyance rose upward within Jesse's chest and he couldn't prevent a note of irritation from filling his voice. He didn't have time for such nonsense. Not if he was going to get the fields cleared for spring planting.

"If you don't do your chores, who will?" Jesse asked, his voice stern but not overly unkind. "Do you want our hens to stop laying eggs? And what about the cows? They need to eat too. Do you want them to stop giving milk? Then what will we eat? What will we have to sell so we can live?"

Jesse didn't really expect a response and he got none. But he hoped his questions would make Sam think. After all, the boy was still young and learning his place in the world. This was a teaching opportunity. A time to reiterate Jesse's expectations and let Sam understand that he needed the boy's help.

"Unless you are at school, you will do your farm chores first and read only in the evenings after all the work is finished for the day. Except on Sunday, we have no time for reading during daytime. Do you understand?"

Sam didn't look up but he nodded. The boy's back was ramrod straight, his shoulders tensed. Jesse sensed the child was upset by the situation but he offered no argument.

"*Gut.* Now, go and get your shoes and coat on. Then, finish your work. After that, come and join me in the south pasture so we can clear the field."

Expecting his son to obey, Jesse turned and headed toward the barn without a backward glance. Because he hadn't purchased any draft horses yet, he harnessed Blaze, his road horse, to the wagon and headed out to the field with his hand tools.

Using a sharp spade to dig around the roots of small trees and shrubs, he worked alone for almost two hours. Even though the day was quite cold, he wiped the sweat from his brow. He dug, hacked and pulled up a number of slender saplings and tossed them into the back of the wagon. He could turn them into wood chips for use around the farm. Marvin

Schwartz had a gas-powered wood chipper he could use for a minimal fee.

Resting for a moment, Jesse leaned against the wooden handle of his tool and reached for the jug of water he'd placed in the back of the wagon. He looked toward the house, wondering where Sam was. Surely the boy was finished with his chores by now. He wouldn't dare go back inside the house to read some more. Would he?

Stowing the water jug behind the wagon seat, Jesse continued his work. He wasn't pleased to see thistles growing in the field and knew they'd be stubborn to get rid of. As an experienced farmer, he knew it would take two or three years to clear them out completely and even then, he'd still have to watch out for new seedlings. But over time, he'd weed them out entirely. A variety of other obnoxious grasses and thug plants would sprout up as well. But effective farming was a patient man's chore. And Jesse was an effective farmer. Within a few years, his farm would be tidy and in optimal working condition. He'd work hard and build a fine place for Sam to inherit one day.

Speaking of which, where was the boy? He looked toward the house again, wondering if he should tromp back to the barn to search for him. He'd never known his son to be so recalcitrant. What had gotten into him?

Setting his tools aside, Jesse stepped over the uneven ground and headed toward the house. It was long past lunchtime and he needed to take a break. Before they returned to the field, he'd fix him and

Sam some sandwiches. While they ate, he'd explain the merits of hard work to his son and encourage the boy to do better. If he found Sam reading again, he'd have to punish him. It was his duty as an Amish father to correct poor behaviors. He'd reprimanded Sam once but the next time would require harsher action. And Jesse didn't look forward to that. No, not at all.

"Sam! Are you here?" he called when he stepped inside the kitchen door.

No answer. He shouted again but still no response.

Turning, he walked out to the chicken coop and then to the barn. A large plop of moisture fell from the sky and struck him on the cheek. Yes, it was definitely going to rain.

He yelled again and again, to get the boy's attention. But he couldn't find him. Patches was missing too. Now that was odd. Where had Sam and the puppy gone off to?

Again, Jesse searched every room of the house. He peered into every stall in the barn, the shed and chicken coop. Where was his son?

And then, a thought occurred to him. Sam hadn't spoken but Jesse knew he'd been upset by the scolding he'd given him that morning. Was it possible Sam had run away? And if so, where would the boy go?

Several heavy raindrops struck Jesse on the face and hand. Soon, the sky would open up its waterworks. And Sam would be caught out in this storm.

Jesse ran to the field, a surge of panic rushing through his veins. He unharnessed Blaze from the wagon and led the horse back to the barn where he hitched him up to the buggy. By the time Jesse steered the horse out of the farmyard, a light mist was falling steadily from the sky.

As he reached the county road, Jesse noticed the rain increased in intensity. Great, heavy drops of water smattered against the windshield of his buggy and he was grateful to be inside, away from the damp and the wind. But his son was out in this storm some-where. Possibly frightened and cold.

Jesse wiped his brow, filled with trepidation. His six-year-old son was all alone. Hopefully, the boy had worn his hat and coat but it didn't matter. Not if the child got wet. If Sam was out in this frigid air for very long, he could easily become sick. And that thought terrorized Jesse. Because he'd already lost the rest of his *familye*. He couldn't lose Sam too.

Maybe the boy had walked over to the Fishers' farm. Maybe he'd sought refuge with Becca. It wasn't far. That's where Jesse would check first. He hoped and prayed his son was inside her house, safe and warm. Because Jesse refused to contemplate any-thing less. He had to find his son. He had to find him right now!

Becca clicked her tongue and urged her cousin's horse onto the county road. Driving the buggy, she'd left the town library and was eager to get home. It was late afternoon and several heavy raindrops thumped against the windshield. It was just a matter of minutes before it started pouring cats and dogs. Though she hadn't wanted to go into town this Satur-day, her trip had been fruitful. Sitting beside her on the cushioned seat was a terrific book on skits that would help augment the year-end school program. She'd also checked out several new books for Sam. Wouldn't he be surprised when she gave them to him on Monday morning at school? He'd read all the other books she'd given him at least twice already.

More raindrops spattered the window and she blinked, thinking her eyes deceived her. Was that Sam walking along the side of the road? He was all alone, his shoulders hunched against the drizzling rain, his head bowed low beneath his black felt hat. Definitely an Amish boy. She couldn't see his face clearly but knew Sam's body build and the way he walked.

Tugging on the lead lines, she pulled the horse over onto the shoulder of the road. The boy side-stepped the buggy and looked up in surprise. She saw that he was carrying Patches, his little black dog, in his arms. He was trying to shield the pup from the driving rain.

What on earth was he doing out here all alone on this busy road in the freezing rain?

She opened the door and called to him. "*Hallo*, Sam. Where are you going?"

He shrugged and blinked in the rain as he scuffed his booted foot against a rock. Patches squirmed in his arms and the boy tightened his hold. His cheeks were rosy from the cold air and he hunched his back against the lashing wind.

"Do you need a ride?" she asked.

He hesitated, then shook his head. But that didn't deter her. This boy was always quiet but she'd learned to read his mannerisms. He was cold and upset. From his red eyes, she could tell he'd been crying. And then, she noticed a little bag slung across his shoulder. A plethora of questions hammered her mind all at once. Was he running away? And why would he do that? Where was he going? Did Jesse know?

Regardless, a six-year-old boy was too young to be out in this rain all alone.

The deluge increased, beating against them like a drum. It gave her the incentive to force her hand.

"Sam, get in the buggy, please. You don't want Patches to catch a bad cold, do you?"

Her reasoning got through to the boy. Thankfully, he did as she asked. If she was reading his expression correctly, it was one of relief. And no wonder. When she opened the door wide and he stepped inside and sat on the seat, he was shivering and his teeth chattered. Patches wasn't in much better shape. The little dog gave a good shake to get the water off before curling next to her side.

"You're both frozen clear through." She reached for the warm quilt her cousin kept stowed on the back seat. After draping it over Sam and Patches, she tucked the edges around them both before rubbing the boy's arms briskly.

"What are you doing so far from home in this storm?" she asked, not really expecting an answer.

He glanced up, his big, brown eyes filled with so much misery that she made a sad little sound in the back of her throat. Before she could stop herself, she pulled him close for a tight hug. After a moment, she released him and clicked to the horse to walk on.

"*Ach*, it can't be all that bad, can it? Did you run away from home?" she asked as she drove the horse through the driving rain.

The boy sat close beside her and she was half-surprised when he gave a slight nod. Oh, no! She hated the thought of Jesse and Sam having trouble between them.

"Did you have a disagreement with your *vadder*?" she asked.

He stared down at Patches and gave another nod.

She hesitated, wondering what she could say to make the situation easier.

"Your *vadder* loves you very much. You know that, don't you?" she asked.

He tossed her a doubtful glare and shook his head. Her heart gave a powerful squeeze. For some reason, it hurt her to think that Sam doubted his father's affection.

"Sometimes it isn't easy to honor our *eldre* but it's a commandment from *Gott*. Your *vadder* knows what's best for you and you must obey him in all things," she said.

Sam's forehead crinkled and he stared out the window, at the sheets of water blanketing the buggy. It wasn't long before they arrived at Jesse's farm but he wasn't there. Maybe he was out looking for Sam.

Becca stowed her horse and buggy inside the barn, then hurried to the house with Sam and Patches. While she got a towel to dry off the dog, she sent Sam upstairs to change out of his damp clothes. Then, she built up the fire in the stove. Since it was late afternoon, she took the liberty of fixing Sam something to eat. She found a pound of ground beef in the refrigerator and made a quick casserole. The boy wolfed down the hot food, which told her he hadn't eaten in a while. She also fed the puppy, satisfied when both of them were warm again.

An hour later, the rain let up and Jesse came home. The moment he stepped inside the kitchen, his gaze riveted on Sam. The boy still sat at the table, sipping a cup of hot chocolate. Patches lay on the floor beside the warm stove.

Without a word, Jesse knelt beside Sam and scooped the boy into his arms to hold him close for several long moments. This action alone told Becca he was beyond relieved to find the boy safe. It displayed Jesse's fear and love for his son more than anything else could. But then, Jesse drew back and clutched Sam's upper arms as he gazed into his eyes. Becca could see that Jesse was cold and angry. No doubt he'd been outside in the rain for quite a long time, looking for his son.

"I've been so worried about you. Where have you been?" Jesse asked, his eyes narrowed on the boy.

Sam stared at his hands folded in his lap, his cup of hot chocolate ignored.

"I found him and Patches walking alone along the side of the road. I was worried because they were out in the freezing rain, so I brought them home," Becca supplied.

Jesse gave a stiff nod. "*Danke* for bringing them home."

"You're *willkomm*." She spoke in a cheery voice, hoping to alleviate some of the tension in the air.

It didn't help. Jesse rounded on Sam again, his face tense with annoyance. He swept his black felt hat off his head and tossed it onto the table before wiping his damp face with an impatient hand. Like his son, his cheeks were pink from the cold and his heavy wool coat was soaked clear through.

"Do you know how worried I was when I found you missing? I had to leave my work and spent most of the afternoon searching for you. I don't have time to go traipsing all over the valley looking for you because you'd rather read your books than do your morning chores. It is not right for you to throw a temper tantrum and run away."

Standing in front of the sink, Becca held very still. Was that what this was all about? Sam had been reading instead of doing his work? Oh, dear. No wonder Jesse was upset. Any Amish father would feel the same way. A disobedient son who didn't do his chores put the entire *familye* at risk. Jesse would be derelict in his parental duties if he didn't reprimand the boy.

"Go to your room now and get ready for bed. I'll be up to collect your books in a few minutes. Except for school and bedtime, there will be no reading in this house for a week," Jesse said.

Something cold gripped Becca's heart. Would Jesse really ground the boy from reading for an entire week?

Sam nodded in obedience as he slid out of his chair and left the room in a rush. Patches padded after him. When they were gone, Becca looked at Jesse, finding his expression grim and forbidding.

"Surely you won't keep the boy from reading, will you? He's been making such great progress. It's his one true enjoyment," she said in a quiet voice.

He looked at her as if he had forgotten she was there. "He's got to learn that work comes before pleasure. He's reading so much that it's interfering with his chores on the farm. He didn't do any of his tasks this morning. And when I chastised him for it, he threw a tantrum and ran away. I wasted an entire afternoon looking for him. He must learn to obey."

"I'm sorry that happened, Jesse. But I'm certain, if you reason with him, he'll understand and want to do better. He's just seeking your approval. He wants your love so much." She held out a pleading hand, her voice gentle and nonconfrontational.

Jesse snorted. "He'll win my approval by obeying what I say. I won't have him reading books instead of doing his chores again. The livestock must not suffer because of his dereliction."

She nodded. "*Ja*, I agree. But maybe if you weren't so grouchy with him all the time, he might be more willing to obey. It's entirely appropriate to reprove your child with sharpness but then if you'd show an increase in love toward him afterward, he might not consider you to be his enemy. As it is, he thinks you don't love him. And I'm sure that's not the message you want to send him."

Jesse shrugged out of his damp coat. His eyes narrowed, his lips pursing tight with disapproval. "Miss Graber, do you presume to tell me how to raise my *sohn*?"

She blinked. "*Ach*, of course not. But it seems you need some help right now. I just thought…"

"I don't need your advice on how to handle my boy," he cut her off.

She stared at him, completely aghast. Of all the nerve! Who did he think he was?

The answer came loud and sharp to her mind. He was Sam's father. She was simply the boy's teacher and didn't have a right to tell Jesse how to raise his own child.

"This isn't your business and I won't allow you to interfere." Jesse's voice was low but powerful, like the sound of rolling thunder off in the distance. His hands were clenched, his features tight.

Some inner guidance told her not to challenge him right now. But she didn't have to like it.

"All right. If that's the way you want it," she said.

Drawing herself up straight, she reached for her scarf and shawl, which lay over the back of one of the kitchen chairs. Without speaking, she jerked them on, wrapping up tight against the frigid wind outside. It had stopped raining but the ride home would undoubtedly be as chilly as it was inside this kitchen.

She walked to the door, longing to say something more. Wishing she dared plead with him to show some compassion toward his son. Sam seemed so lost right now. So did Jesse.

He didn't speak as she stepped out onto the back porch. A blast of chilly wind struck her in the face and she gasped. It slapped the screen door closed behind her. It reminded her of the glacial man standing inside, watching her go.

He didn't walk outside to see that she was safely in her buggy and on her way. But as she pulled out of the yard, she saw him standing at the living room window, watching her with a severe expression on his face. If she hadn't seen his deep concern for Sam, she might think he hated the boy. That he hated the world.

She tried to calm her trembling hands and beating heart as she headed home. She told herself everything was all right. Sam was safe. Jesse was obviously upset but, in the morning, things would look differently. Jesse would calm down and so would Sam. Unfortunately, the problem wouldn't just resolve itself. Deep in her heart, she knew the issue wasn't going away anytime soon. It occurred to her that Jesse's trust in *Gott* was in tatters. He hadn't said so but she knew without asking. His faith had been greatly damaged. And though she longed to help him and Sam, she had no idea how to go about it. Other than to keep tutoring Sam and trying to show both of them compassion, she didn't have a clue. She just hoped it was enough.

Chapter Ten

Sam didn't show up for school Monday morning. A part of Becca wondered if it was because of the disagreement she'd had with Jesse when the child ran away. Another part of her thought it might be just because Jesse was so busy with work that he couldn't drive the boy here. She thought of offering to pick Sam up every morning on her way. After all, they lived only a mile apart. But she was already tutoring the boy three afternoons each week and barely keeping up with her own work as it was. It also occurred to her that Jesse needed that time alone with Sam each day, to be a father. What he did with the time was up to him. He could make it a quality chat with his boy or a silent, sullen trip.

Deciding not to make more out of Sam's absence than necessary, she taught her lessons as usual. As she worked with the fourth-graders and Caleb Yoder, she couldn't believe the difference in him. Since that second week when she'd started teaching here, he'd been so good and helpful. Maybe his older brother and sister had told on him and Bishop Yoder had corrected Caleb's poor behavior. Whatever it was, Becca was grateful. Now, the school was quiet and orderly and she really thought she was making headway with the children.

That afternoon, she set aside Sam's work and waited until all the other children had left for the day. Then, she loaded her books into her buggy and drove over to Jesse's farm to tutor Sam as usual. The day was cool but the sky was clear and the sun was shining. That was a good sign that spring was on its way.

She parked beside Jesse's house and knocked on the front door. Glancing at the flowerbeds, she noticed the tulips and daffodils had poked their heads out of the soil. The last church service had focused on Easter and the Savior's resurrection, reminding her to carry hope within her heart. Another month and school would be out for the summer. But that thought caused a brief surge of panic to rise in Becca's throat. The last day of school was on May first. One more month and she would have to leave or find work elsewhere. But where would she go? She'd been sending job inquiries to numerous Amish communities across the nation and received not one positive response. Her common sense told her to doubt the future but then she reminded herself to have faith.

The door creaked open and Sam peered out at her with his big, dark eyes. When he saw her, he thrust open the door and threw himself at her in a tight hug.

"*Ach, hallo*, Sam! I missed you at school today. Are you ill?" she asked, determined to be positive and act like he'd never run away. It must be a bit embarrassing to him and his father and it would serve no purpose in bringing it up again. After all, it really wasn't her business.

He released her and stood in the living room, looking down at his stockinged feet as he shook his head. Except for shoes, he was fully dressed but his hair was rumpled and he had holes in his woolen socks where his little toes poked through. No doubt Jesse didn't have time to mend the socks for him. And once again, she was reminded with glaring clarity that this little boy badly needed a mother.

"Then why didn't you *komm* to school today?" she asked in a light tone.

He just shrugged and stepped back so she had room to come inside.

Becca set her bag on the floor, noticing a new sofa and coffee table perched in front of the wide window. They were drab brown and plain but appeared comfortable enough.

"These are nice," she said.

Sam didn't respond but she really didn't expect him to.

A Bible and some of Sam's books sat on top of the table. Gas lights had been installed in each corner of the room. The added illumination brightened the room and even seemed more cheerful inside. Gradually, Jesse was creating a pleasant home to live in. He was trying to pick up the pieces of his life.

So was she. But it wasn't easy. For any of them. And that's when she realized Jesse wasn't the only one who had trust issues. So did she. Vernon's betrayal had made her feel unacceptable, like she didn't belong anywhere. As if she wasn't worthy of love.

Her hands trembled slightly as she reached inside her bag and pulled out the assignments Sam had missed that day. She would catch him up on that first, then proceed to his reading and coax him to answer her questions out loud. If he got it all done this afternoon, she would mark him down as attending school today and his attendance wouldn't be marred by any absences. She wanted that for him so she could give him a special certificate at the end of the year, to help build his self-confidence.

"Let's start with our English, shall we?" she suggested.

She set a McGuffey reader on the coffee table and scooted over on the new sofa to give Sam room to join her. She was pleased when he read several sentences out loud to her, though he still spoke in a soft whisper she could barely hear. But it was great progress when she considered where they'd started a couple of months earlier.

They had just finished their phonics and were starting on penmanship when she heard the back door open and close.

"What are you doing here?"

She looked up. Jesse stood in the kitchen doorway. His hair was slightly damp around his face and neck and she thought he must have washed up in the barn. The dust on his broadfall pants and shirt attested that he'd worked hard that day. He lifted a hand to brace against the doorjamb, looking genuinely surprised to see her here. Did he think she was so shallow that she'd stay away simply because they'd disagreed on the best way to handle Sam's running away? If so, Jesse didn't know her very well.

"I came to tutor Sam, of course," she said, feeling a bit offended by his question.

He glanced at the books, his eyes crinkled in confusion. "I... I didn't think you'd *komm* back after the argument we had."

He certainly was blunt, she'd give him that. He never seemed to hold anything back.

She snorted. "Of course I would. Sam needs help. I would never punish him because you're being so bull-headed."

She turned her attention back to Sam, thinking she shouldn't have said that. But maybe it was something Jesse needed to hear. Handing Sam a pencil, she kept her head bowed and focused on the child's work. He wrote several words on his big, ruled paper and she took every opportunity to praise him.

"Very *gut*. Your letters are so legible. You're getting better at writing every day," she said.

Sam showed a shy smile and wrote some more words. When she looked up again, Jesse was gone. She could hear him inside the kitchen, rattling pots around. No doubt he was scrounging up something for his and Sam's supper.

She thought of going to help. She knew Jesse wasn't much of a cook. But no. He was Sam's father. He needed to serve his son. It was his job to provide for the boy. And besides, he needed to learn that he couldn't treat people rudely. Not if he expected to have any friends. It was better to leave him alone and let him come to these realizations on his own. But a part of her dearly wished she could be his friend too.

"*Ach*, it looks like you've got everything under control here. Whatever you're cooking smells *gut*."

Jesse turned and found Becca standing in the kitchen doorway. She had already put on her heavy shawl, gloves and scarf…ready to leave. She sniffed the air and breathed a little sigh for emphasis. Her voice sounded jolly and she was smiling. He stared at her for several seconds, wishing she wasn't so cheerful all the time. It made it harder not to like her.

"Are you finished teaching Sam for the night?" he asked, turning back to the stove.

He had just finished frying several ground beef patties without burning them and planned to cover them with hot cream of mushroom soup. It was called poor man's steak and had been a staple from his childhood. A baked potato, string beans and canned pears would round out the meal. He even had whipped up some chocolate pudding for dessert. Sam would like that.

"*Ja*, Sam does better every day," she said. "He's made a tremendous amount of progress. I'm even hopeful he'll speak his part out loud for the end-of-year program. He's told me he wants to. I just hope he isn't too nervous when the time comes."

She stepped over to the stove and watched him whisk the mushroom gravy around in the meat drippings. He thought about inviting her to stay for supper but decided against it. For some reason, this woman made him feel nervous. He couldn't think clearly when she was standing so near. Besides, they were both single and it was getting late. She needed to go home. Right now.

Lifting the pan, he set it on a hot pad in the middle of the table. Alice would have poured it into a bowl with a ladle and made their meal as dignified as possible. But he didn't have time for such nonsense. After supper, he must return to the barn. His road horse had thrown a shoe so he couldn't take Sam to school that morning. He needed to use the animal out in the fields tomorrow, which meant the shoe must be replaced tonight. He really needed to buy some draft horses. Then he wouldn't have to use his road horse in the fields.

He reached for a dish towel to wipe his hands… a nervous gesture to give himself something to do. Again, he glanced at Becca, expecting her to leave. "Was there something else you needed?"

She shook her head, meeting his gaze. "*Ne*, I just wanted to apologize for the harsh words I said to you a couple of days ago. I fear I'm too bold at times and may have caused offense and that wasn't my intention."

"I'm sorry too." He spoke the words before he could think to stop himself. Their argument had been on his mind since it happened and he wanted to clear the air.

Her expression softened and she smiled. "*Danke.* I know you're doing your best with Sam and you were worried about him that day. Fear can cause us to say things we don't really mean. But you're doing a really *gut* job with him."

Her insight impressed him. It was as if she could see deep inside of him and knew exactly what he was thinking. The only other person to do that had been Alice.

"It's kind of difficult for me to admit when I'm wrong," he said. "I was raised by a rather stern *vadder*. He was always right even when he was wrong. He was a *gut* man but very stubborn. There was little laughter in my home when I was growing up. I've tried not to be that way. My wife taught me that apologies make us stronger. I didn't mean to come across as unfeeling toward my *sohn*."

He spoke the words slowly, surprised at how painful it was for him to make the admission. Although his father had taught him a strong work ethic and how to farm, most of the memories from his youth were not pleasant. And he wasn't sure why he was telling Becca this. She was way too easy to confide in. Too easy to be with. But he knew in his heart of hearts that he must apologize to her. He was trying so hard to start anew. For some reason, it was highly important to him not to have conflict with Sam's teacher. Mostly because she'd been good to him and Sam and they owed her a debt of gratitude. But he sensed there was another reason too. Something he didn't understand.

"*Ach*, just because the horse bucks you off doesn't mean you sell the horse," she said. "The Savior taught us to have a soft heart filled with humility. And when we are filled with His love, we are quick to forgive. But it can still be a hard thing to do. For all of us."

Hmm. Again, her insight surprised him. Just like Alice, it seemed that Becca was teaching him some rather difficult lessons. Her patient reminder of the Savior helped him realize he could learn a lot from this good woman.

"I've been meaning to ask, would you be willing to teach a fire safety class at school next week?" she asked suddenly.

Jesse stared at her, his mouth dropping open in surprise. Because of his past, he wasn't certain he felt up to the task. He couldn't do it. Could he?

"I… I'm not sure I'm the right person to do that," he said, trying not to sound insecure.

"Why not? You're a certified firefighter. It must have taken a lot of study and effort to master that skill. You must be very *gut* at it. And it's an interesting profession we can highlight for the *kinder*. You're a *gut* example of a *vadder* who has reached out to help his community."

He didn't know how to respond. He didn't feel like a good father. How could he explain to this dedicated woman that he hadn't been able to fight fire ever since he'd lost his wife and daughters? Even now, he hated to add kindling to the stove in his own home. Every time he saw the flames, he thought about losing Alice and their girls.

"Do you feel reluctant because of how your *familye* died?" she asked, her voice achingly soft and gentle.

Wow! She really did lay it out in the open, no mincing words. And yet, hearing his own thoughts spoken out loud made his fears seem a little less threatening.

He ducked his head, a hard lump forming in his throat. He hated to show any weakness to this woman and fought to regain control. When he felt her hand on his arm, he looked into her eyes. She stood so close, her face creased with compassion.

"I know losing part of your *familye* must have been so difficult for you, Jesse. But for Sam's sake and also your own, you have to go on living. From what I've heard at church, you were *gut* at fighting fires. Who better to teach the scholars about fire safety? The people of our *Gmay* could really benefit from your skill too. I hope you'll think about it. You can let me know your decision tomorrow morning, when you bring Sam to school."

She turned and walked toward the back door, the heels of her practical black shoes tap-tapping against the wooden floor. He didn't turn to watch her leave but he heard the door close behind her.

Teach fire safety at school?

He couldn't do it. And yet, Becca's gentle encouragement made him feel like he could do anything. But surely not that. Then again, it had been over a year since the house fire. He used to love fighting fires. Used to love helping people save their homes and businesses. Until he'd lost his wife and daughters, he'd felt like he was doing something good for his community. That he was helping his Amish people save their houses and barns too. Maybe it was time to put aside his grief and take it up again. Maybe...

But what if he did something wrong? What if he panicked and made a mistake? He couldn't stand the thought of losing someone else on his watch. Especially someone he cared deeply about.

Becca thought he could do it. She seemed to really believe in him. She was counting on him. And it felt so good to be needed again. So good to have someone in his life that he could talk to about Sam and all that he had lost. Maybe he should think about it a little more.

Chapter Eleven

Becca arrived at school early the following morning. With no snow to shovel, she was able to get the classroom warmed up and set out her lesson plans before the scholars arrived. Then, she went outside to welcome each child. And when Jesse pulled into the schoolyard, she helped Sam hop out of the buggy and leaned in to greet the boy's father.

"*Guder mariye*, Jesse!" she called, purposefully trying to be pleasant.

"*Hallo,*" he said, not returning her smile.

Sam hugged Becca, then ran off to meet Andy Yoder, who had just walked into the schoolyard with his brothers and sisters. Although Andy did most of the talking, Becca had seen Sam speaking a few words to the other boy on rare occasion. Andy was the same age as Sam and the two had become good friends. Just another subtle reminder that Sam was doing better and much happier at school.

Turning back to Jesse, she showed a smile of encouragement. "Have you thought more about teaching a fire safety class to the *kinder*?"

He gripped the leather lead lines and frowned, seeming a bit pensive. Maybe she shouldn't push him so hard. But the alternative was that she would have to teach the class and she thought it would be more effective coming from a firefighter.

"*Ja*, I will do it," he said.

"*Wundervoll!*" she exclaimed. "Will next Monday, first thing in the morning, work for you? Then you can leave right afterward and we won't take up too much of your day."

He nodded. "That will work but I'll need at least two hours to teach a proper safety class."

She blinked. "So much time?"

He nodded. "*Ja*, to do it correctly."

Hmm. Being Amish, she took fire for granted. After all, her people used it in their everyday life to heat their homes and cook their food. But she wanted to do this right. Maybe the schoolchildren had learned bad habits in building fires. Learning some safety techniques might make a difference for one of them at some time in their life. It might make a difference for her as well.

"*Allrecht.* You can have all the time you need," she said.

"I'll plan on two hours. But just one other thing. Don't start a fire in the stove that morning and I'll show the *kinder* the proper way to clean up a cold fire and how to prepare it for burning."

"*Ja*, I'll remember. And *danke!*"

She closed the door and stepped back. He tugged

on the brim of his straw hat and gave her a slight smile before he slapped the leads against the horse's rump. And for some odd reason, his smile meant everything to her.

The buggy pulled away and she watched him go. A sense of exhilaration filled her as she entered the school and taught lessons to the scholars. She felt inordinately happy today and didn't understand why. Maybe it was because the sun was shining, the tulips were peeking out from the chilled soil and Sam had a friend and was doing better in school. Caleb Yoder had taken the younger boy under his wing and was reading to him several times each day. Jesse had agreed to teach the fire safety class and had even smiled at her that morning. Not even the impending monthly school board meeting later that afternoon could diminish her spirits. The meeting was held on the first Tuesday of every month. Becca had already reminded the scholars and they were prepared for the visit.

The day passed quickly and she felt organized when Bishop Yoder, Mervin Schwartz and Darrin Albrecht came inside, a little bit early. They each removed their black felt hats as they entered the school. Their wives were with them, Mervin's wife holding their two-year-old daughter in her arms. A couple of other parents filtered in as well. They didn't interrupt the class as they quietly sat at the back of the room but the students were highly aware that they had guests.

Becca was leaning over Susan Hostetler, helping the girl sound out a particularly difficult word, when the door opened again. Glancing up, she saw Jesse King standing there, his gaze resting on her. And instantly, her face heated up like a road flare. She felt as if everyone in the room was watching her. What was Jesse doing here? Any of their people were invited to attend the school board meetings but he'd never participated before. And they'd just spoken that morning. So, what reason did he have to be here now?

He reached up and removed his straw hat, glancing around the room for a place to sit. Bishop Yoder motioned to him and he sauntered over to sit nearby, his legs overly long in the small desk.

Becca ducked her head further over Susan's reading book, hoping no one noticed her hot cheeks. She scolded herself, remembering to act professional. She had no idea why Jesse affected her like this. He was just the parent of one of her students. That was all. Nothing more.

Standing straight, she moved toward the front of the room, speaking loud enough for everyone to hear. "Scholars, we'd like to *willkomm* our visitors to our school. Will you please put away your studies now and stand at the front of the room?"

There was a slight rustling as the children did as she asked. As usual, they would sing a couple of songs for their guests, then go outside. Some of the children would go home to do their evening chores while others would play in the yard until their parents were ready to leave. They'd been rehearsing their songs and Becca had reminded them of the board meeting earlier that morning, so they were prepared.

She stood beside her desk, waiting for the scholars to line up with the oldest and tallest students in the back and the younger children in the front. They all looked so earnest, eager and innocent as they waited for her signal. And she loved each and every one of them. How she would miss them when the school year ended and she had to leave to find employment elsewhere.

Lifting her hand, she hummed a note to give them their starting key, then led them in two German songs. Their voices rang out in unison, sweet and melodious. Out of her peripheral vision, she saw Jesse watching his son with unblinking eyes. The man's countenance was one of rapt attention and appreciation. In spite of his gruffness, she knew he loved the little boy very much.

The other parents in the room wore similar expressions. Like any caring parent, they adored their children. And a quiet pain settled within Becca's chest. Yes, she'd chosen the teaching profession. It was a career she hoped to embrace and excel at. One that would support her financially throughout her life. But teaching was also a labor of love. She took her responsibilities seriously, to mold her young scholars into upstanding Amish people. But a part of her ached with emptiness. All her life, she had hoped to marry a kind, loving man and hold her own children within her arms. Now, it seemed that would never happen. Because Vernon had broken her heart, she didn't dare trust another man again. And at times like this, she had trouble accepting that.

During church the previous Sunday, the sermon

had been out of the Gospel of Matthew. Ask and it shall be given you, seek and ye shall find. It occurred to Becca that, if she wanted to remain in Riverton, she should ask the Lord and exercise faith that He could make it happen.

The last note of the song ended and Becca lowered her arm and smiled at her students. "*Danke*, scholars. You have done well today and are now dismissed from school. I'll see you tomorrow morning."

The children put on their coats and gathered up their bags and lunch pails before racing outside. Their laughter rang through the air as they closed the door behind them.

As if on cue, the school board members stood and walked to the front of the room. With their long beards and black frock coats, the three fathers looked a bit intimidating. As was their habit, they sat facing Becca's desk.

Forcing herself to retain her composure, Becca picked up her notebook and pencil and waited for Bishop Yoder to conduct the meeting. She presented a list of supplies and they discussed a couple of discipline problems.

"I understand my son Caleb has been acting up in school," the bishop said.

Becca nodded. "*Ja*, he and Enos have caused a couple of disturbances in the past."

"They are not causing trouble now?"

"*Ne*, lately they have been *gut* as can be. In fact, I assigned both boys as reading and math partners with some of the younger scholars and they both seem to have taken this task quite seriously. I have had no more problems with either boy for some time now."

"*Gut*. I had heard there was a problem and waited for you to speak with me about it, but you never did," he said.

A moment of confusion filled her mind. Had she made a mistake by not talking to him about it sooner?

"I... I wanted to handle it myself, if possible. And it turns out that everything is fine now. The boys are being very well-behaved."

Hopefully, the board members were impressed enough with how she had handled the situation that they would write her a good teaching recommendation for a future position somewhere else.

"I am happy to hear this news. You are to be commended for how you have dealt with the problem," Bishop Yoder said.

Becca couldn't help feeling pleased by the bishop's praise. Not only did she highly respect this man but she also wanted to do a good job. She desired to help her students become better people.

The other two board members nodded their agreement and Bishop Yoder turned to face the rest of the parents in the room.

"Are there any other issues that need to be brought to our attention?" he asked.

No one spoke but Jesse stood, signaling he wished to make a comment.

"*Ja*, what is it?" Bishop Yoder asked in a kind tone.

"Ahem." Jesse cleared his throat and shifted his booted feet nervously. "I just wanted to say that Miss

Graber has gone out of her way to provide extra tutoring for my Sam. She's done a *wundervoll* job working with him and he's even speaking a little bit now and then. I wanted the school board to know how grateful I am that you hired such a willing, capable teacher for our children."

A couple of the mothers in the room nodded their agreement. Becca stared, completely overwhelmed. She couldn't believe Jesse had gone out of his way to give her a good review. He seemed so harsh. So disapproving and downright difficult at times. And then he went and did something so kind and generous. And just in time too. There was only one month left before school let out for the summer. She was beyond grateful for what he'd done.

"*Danke*. It has been my pleasure to work with Sam and the other scholars. They're great kids and I care deeply for each one of them," she said, retaining her professional demeanor.

And she meant every word. She loved teaching. Loved serving these amazing children. She just wished she could stay in Riverton and teach them next year too. But Caroline Schwartz was out of the hospital and walking with the help of a walker. She'd possibly need the aid of a cane for the rest of her life but she was healing and would be back in the fall. There was no other position for Becca in this community. In order to support herself, she'd have to leave the area.

She'd have to leave Jesse and little Sam too. And though she didn't understand why, that thought made her feel so sad and forlorn that she wanted to cry.

The meeting ended soon after and Jesse slipped out the door before she could catch him to thank him privately for what he'd said. She watched him go, thinking maybe it was for the best. He was still hurting over the deaths of his wife and daughters. He had his hands full with Sam and making a go of his farm. He had no room in his life or his heart for an opinionated schoolteacher like Becca. And yet, she couldn't help wishing he did.

As promised, Jesse arrived early the following Monday to teach the fire safety class. He parked his buggy in the back and Sam helped him carry a couple of fire extinguishers into the schoolhouse. As they crossed the graveled yard, Jesse watched his little son race toward the front door, his arms filled with his lunch pail and a red extinguisher. The boy was smiling, eager to get inside and greet Becca. And Jesse couldn't help thinking how happy his son was lately. In fact, Jesse felt happier too. And though he didn't fully understand why, he sensed that it was partly due to Becca and her gentle influence in their lives.

"*Guder mariye*! I'm so glad you're here." She greeted them with her usual cheery disposition.

Jesse returned her smile. He couldn't help himself. She was depending on him and he wanted to do a good job for her.

"I've cleared the top of my desk, so you have a place to set your things during your presentation." She eyed the two red standard fire extinguishers he held.

"*Danke* but I won't need much room. This is for you. For the schoolhouse." He held one of the extinguishers out to her.

She took it and looked up into his eyes. He felt transfixed by her gaze.

"That's very kind of you," she said, her voice seeming to come from a haze.

He cleared his throat and moved away, trying to focus on the task at hand. Sam set the third fire extinguisher he'd been carrying on top of a desk, then picked up the wood bucket from beside the cold potbellied stove. He hurried outside to collect some firewood and kindling, just as Jesse had asked him to do before they'd arrived.

The students came in, doffing their jackets and placing their lunch pails on the shelf beneath the coatracks. They talked quietly together as they took their seats. Jesse stood silently at the side of the classroom and watched as Becca greeted each and every scholar. She asked them questions pertaining to their lives. One had a new baby sister at home and another one had found an injured starling they were caring for. It seemed she knew everything about these children's lives and took a genuine interest in them.

Sam returned with the wood bucket and set it beside the stove. Jesse was surprised when he waved to Caleb Yoder. The older boy smiled back before sliding into his seat.

Becca stood at the front of the room and folded her hands together as she lifted her chin higher in the air. The children quickly took their seats.

"Scholars, we have a special guest with us today.

Mr. King is a certified firefighter from Pennsylvania. He has agreed to teach us some fire safety techniques. And I know you'll be extra polite and give him your undivided attention." With a satisfied nod, she stepped aside and sat at an empty desk near the front of the room.

Okay, Jesse was on. He cleared his throat and stood, gazing into each earnest face. They seemed so eager to learn. And he couldn't help thinking about the lesson he'd heard at church the day before. The minister had preached from the book of Matthew: Ask and it shall be given you, seek and you shall find. Jesse had been pondering the powerful message ever since. He'd been tempted to speak with Becca about the topic. It seemed he gravitated to her whenever she was near, yet something held him back. His love and loyalty for his wife. His own sense of guilt. Surely the message from the Gospel of Matthew was for other people, not for him. But then again, maybe he was wrong.

"*Danke* for inviting me here today," he said, trying to gather his courage. After all, it had been over a year since he'd had anything to do with the firefighting world and he wasn't sure he was ready for this experience. But no matter. He was here and would do his best.

"The first thing I want to teach you is how to ensure your stove and flue is clean." He stepped over to the cold potbellied stove and pointed at the filled wood bucket Sam had set there just minutes before.

"The wood bucket should never be this close to the stove. It should always be at least two or three arms' lengths away. That way, an errant spark from the stove won't strike the wood that's in the bucket and catch fire."

To emphasize his point, he moved the wood bucket several yards away, to the side of the classroom. Earlier, he had asked Sam to put the bucket right next to the stove so he could make this point. And he was pleased that his son had followed his instructions exactly. He glanced at his boy and found him watching intently. As a way of saying thank you, he smiled and winked at his son. Sam smiled back, looking pleased to have helped.

"Gather around me so you can see how to check the chimney flue to see if it needs cleaning." Jesse beckoned to the students and they instantly did as he asked.

Over the next thirty minutes, Jesse taught them the proper way to check the chimney flue for cleaning and showed them how to adjust the damper so they could control the amount of heat and smoke they got out of the fire.

"At this time of year, it's a bit warmer so you don't need as much heat from the fire. Back east, we used hard woods like oak and maple in our fires. Here in Colorado, we're burning Ponderosa Pine because it's plentiful in the area and easy to gather. But it's a soft wood that burns relatively fast. It's also a heavy soot builder, so the flue needs to be cleaned more frequently. I recommend four times per year," he explained.

The children listened intently to every word he said. When he remembered that first week when

Becca had just started teaching here and he'd entered the school to find the students in absolute chaos, he was impressed by the order she had since established.

As the kids crowded close to see, he held up a book of matches. He was amazed that, without being asked, the older, taller students had put the younger, shorter children closest to him so they could see better. Sam stood nearby, watching his every move.

"When you start a fire inside your house or another building, you should never, ever use an accelerant such as kerosene or gasoline. It can explode out on you and burn you and the entire building. And do not play with matches. They aren't a toy and can burn your entire house down. Don't ever do it! I can't emphasize this enough," he said.

His words were a reminder of what his *familye* had gone through over a year earlier. A hard lump formed in his throat as he knelt before the stove to show the students how to clean out the ashes. When that was done, he discussed the proper way to start a fire and laid some wrinkled newspaper and kindling in the stove. His voice sounded calm and even as he talked but his hands were trembling. Looking up, he saw Becca watching him closely. Her forehead was furrowed and her eyes crinkled in a frown of concern.

Lifting the book of matches, he pulled one from the packet and scraped it across the coarse striking area. A little *whoosh* sounded as the match lit with fire. A commotion came from behind him and he turned, the match going out.

Sam stood there, his eyes wide with terror, his

face contorted in absolute anguish. He had backed up, knocking into two of the older kids. What was wrong with him?

"Sam?" Jesse called.

Had lighting a single match frightened his son? It shouldn't. But even Jesse felt a slight tremor in his arms and legs. Though he started all the fires at his house, he still disliked the chore. And then it dawned on him that Sam was never in the room with him when he started fires at home. Although the child brought in plenty of wood and kindling, he was always absent until the fire was going and the door to the stove was shut.

A small cry escaped Sam's throat. Without explanation, the boy whirled around and pushed through the wall of students. When he finally made his way out into the open area of the classroom, he raced toward the exit. Throwing the door open wide, he ran out into the schoolyard.

Jesse stood, his lesson on fire safety all but forgotten. He was about to run after his son but Becca held out a hand.

"I'll go after him. Please, continue your demonstration," she said.

He blinked in confusion as she hurried after his son. She closed the door behind her. Out of the wide windows surrounding the room, he saw a flash of her skirts as she ran behind the building.

A sniffle brought his attention back to the students. They stared at him in confusion, their eyes wide with worry.

"Is Sam gonna be *allrecht*, Mr. King?" little Andy Yoder asked.

Jesse showed a confident smile he didn't feel. "*Ja*, he'll be fine. Don't worry. Now, let's continue with our lesson."

He put his thoughts on involuntary reflex, discussing the fire extinguishers he'd brought and how the children should aim them at the base of the flame. Then, he taught them how to recognize the exits of a building and escape a burning room in orderly fashion rather than panicking and trampling one another underfoot. He had them each get down low to the floor where they could breathe fresh air when smoke filled the room so they could crawl toward the exit. Then, he took them outside to teach them how to properly dispose of the ashes from their fires.

Out in the schoolyard, he looked around for some sign of Becca and Sam. He saw them some distance away, sitting on the banks of the creek that meandered past the bishop's property. Hearing his voice, they stood and Becca held Sam's hand as the two of them rejoined the group of students. Sam's eyes were red from crying and he wouldn't meet Jesse's eyes. Instead, the boy stared at the ground. An overwhelming urge to take his little boy into his arms and comfort him swept over Jesse. In the past, he would have resisted. But not now. Not today. Becca had taught Jesse to have more compassion. He didn't need to be as stern as his father had been with him.

Interrupting his lecture, he swept his son into his arms and hugged him tight, whispering in his ear for his hearing alone.

"It's going to be okay, *sohn*. I love you," Jesse said.

Hearing his words, Sam softened in his arms. Jesse set the boy back on his feet next to Becca. She nodded her approval as he returned to his lesson. His heart felt a bit lighter and he knew he'd done the right thing by showing some affection toward Sam. If nothing else, it showed the boy that he wasn't angry with him.

"If there's a fire in the schoolhouse, do you have an assigned place to gather outside so your teacher can count you and know that everyone got out safely?" he asked the group.

The children gazed at him with blank expressions.

"*Ne*, but we will assign a place right now," Becca said. "What about right here where we are standing in the middle of the play area?"

Jesse shook his head, a feeling of gratitude filling his heart. Though he pretended to act normal, he was beyond grateful to Becca for helping him with Sam.

"This isn't a *gut* place. It's too close to the schoolhouse. I suggest you meet over here, far away from any potentially burning structures." He walked over to the baseball diamond and stood on the home plate.

"*Ja*, I see what you mean. This is an open area, far away from any buildings, where we can easily be seen," Becca said.

"*Ach*, so where will you meet outside if the school is ever on fire?" he asked the students in a booming voice.

"Here!" they responded in unison.

"Very *gut*. Now, one last lesson and then I'll leave

you for the day. I want to discuss the proper way to dispose of the ashes from your stove," he said.

As they walked behind the schoolhouse to a safe fire circle that had been set up specifically for this task, he showed them how to stir the ashes around with a bit of water but not bury them since that would bank the heat inside and keep the fire alive. He taught them how to feel carefully with the back of their hands to ensure no warmth came from the ashes. And only then could they be assured that there were no live coals that could spring to life and be carried by the wind to start a wildfire burning. And by the time he had finished the training, he was no longer shaking. Sam was smiling again too.

"Scholars, what do you say to Mr. King?" Becca asked the students when Jesse had finished his lecture.

They all smiled and responded together. "*Danke*, Mr. King."

He nodded, feeling relieved to have this chore finished. *"Gaern gscheh."*

"Scholars, please return to the classroom and prepare for reading time. I'm going to have a private word with Mr. King and will come inside in just a few minutes," she said.

A couple of snickers from the students accompanied her comment and she looked to see who it came from. But all the students looked completely innocent as they turned and walked back to the schoolhouse.

"*Danke* again for your very thorough lesson," she said.

She accompanied him to his horse and buggy. He felt drained of emotion for some reason and thought it must be because he'd faced a fear that had been haunting him for months now.

"Do you think Sam will be all right?" she asked. "He wouldn't tell me what was wrong."

"*Ja*, he'll be fine. I'll spend extra time with him this evening. I… I better let you get back to your school," he said. His emotions swirled around inside of him in a mass of confusion. He felt better but he also felt worse at the same time. He didn't need to ask Sam what was wrong to understand what the boy was feeling.

"*Ja*, I better get back." She stepped away, her lips and cheeks a pretty shade of pink.

"I'll see you later this afternoon when you come to tutor Sam." He spoke as he stepped into the buggy.

She didn't speak but merely waved. Then, she took off at a slight jog toward the schoolhouse.

He watched her go, thinking today was completely unexpected. When he'd arrived here this morning, he hadn't expected Sam's actions or his own response to the fire safety class. His feelings were a riot of unease. Becca probably thought he was crazy. He wished he could open his heart and let her in. But there was still one glaring problem. She wasn't Alice. And she never would be.

Chapter Twelve

The day of the box social arrived too soon. When Becca had first moved to Riverton, the school board had asked her to schedule the event as a fund-raiser so they could buy a teeter-totter and other playground equipment. It wasn't difficult. Just a few announcements made at church and some reminders sent home with the children. The bishop had agreed to let her borrow the benches and tables used by the congregation and the members of the *Gmay* provided the labor to set them up. She just hoped it was a success.

"It's a beautiful day for the social." Hannah Schwartz handed a roll of masking tape to Becca.

She glanced at the azure sky, grateful they wouldn't be rained out. "*Ja*, we couldn't ask for more."

She pulled off a piece of tape and spread it across the corner of the plastic tablecloth to hold it down so the wind wouldn't blow it off. Standing in the schoolyard, she gazed at the other folding tables and chairs they had set up earlier that morning. It was Saturday afternoon and they were almost ready to begin. With the sun shining, they were sure to have a good turnout. But she couldn't help feeling a bit melancholy. Even if they earned enough funds for the playground equipment today, she'd never get to see it. With just two weeks of school left, she'd soon be cleaning out the classroom and packing her things for her trip back home to Ohio. Hopefully, she'd have a glowing letter of recommendation in her purse. She must have faith that *Gott* had her best interests at heart and would guide her through life.

Deciding not to wallow in self-pity, she turned and picked up a stack of bread baskets. They also belonged to the *Gmay*. Since they held so many social events, the investment was well worth it.

Abby, Aunt Naomi, Sarah Yoder and Linda Hostetler were setting out vases of tulips and daffodils picked from their own yards as centerpieces for each table. Bishop Yoder and Darrin Albrecht were unloading a propane barbecue off the back of a wagon. Their teenaged sons helped lift the heavy weight. Since bidding was usually reserved for the adults and older teenagers, each *familye* had been instructed to bring side dishes and desserts to feed their children. More people were arriving, hurrying to lend a hand as they prepared for the fun occasion.

"How does the box table look?"

Becca turned and found Lizzie and Eli Stoltzfus standing behind her. The couple was newly married and Lizzie was just far enough along in her first pregnancy that she was glowing with happiness.

Eli pointed to the table they'd set up for displaying the boxed suppers. The women and some of the girls of the *Gmay* had each decorated a cardboard box with newspaper and tulips and filled it with a dinner for two. Except for the size of each box, they looked almost identical. Later, the men would bid on the boxes in anticipation of eating a meal with one of their womenfolk. Generally the boxes were kept anonymous, so the men wouldn't know whose they were bidding on. But sometimes, people dropped hints in order to rig the bidding so the single couples could eat together. At least, that was their hope.

For just a moment, Becca wished Jesse might buy her box. But she pushed that thought aside. His heart belonged to a dead woman and that was that.

A white cloth had been spread across the box table and Lizzie had pinned yellow and red tulips and daffodils along the edge to give it a special flair. They had already set the boxed dinners strategically on the table, to catch the eyes of the male bidders. Becca could see her own box sitting toward the back, decorated with sheets of newspaper and two red tulips affixed on top.

"*Ach*, the table looks beautiful!" Becca exclaimed.

"How about if we have the bidding on the boxes first? Then I can fire up the grill to cook for the *kinder* and other people who won't be bidding on a box." Bishop Yoder spoke from nearby.

"That sounds great. I'll leave that to you," Becca said.

Though she'd never seen him in action, she'd been told the bishop was a good auctioneer. And she was happy to coordinate everything and let him handle the business end of the occasion.

At that moment, Jesse and Sam's buggy pulled into the yard. Becca's senses went on high alert. She returned Sam's energetic wave but forced herself not to run over to greet them. She didn't want to look too forward. Not with almost everyone in the *Gmay* watching.

Children raced past and adults laughed together as everyone arrived in time for the bidding. Becca kept herself busy laying out stacks of paper plates, cups and napkins. She had no idea who would bid on her basket and hoped they liked fried chicken.

"Everyone! Gather round and we'll have a blessing on the food. Then, we'll start the bidding." Standing on a raised wooden platform, the bishop waved his arms and spoke in a booming voice to get everyone's attention.

The people stepped forward in anticipation. Some of the teenaged boys eyed the decorated boxes, bending their heads together and pointing as they speculated on who had made them. Glancing up, Becca saw Abby chatting with Jesse as she bounced little Chrissie on her hip.

Hmm. Abby wouldn't tell him which box belonged to her, would she? Both Abby and Aunt Naomi had been in the kitchen when Becca had packed and decorated her box, so they definitely knew which one was hers.

They bowed their heads and blessed the food. Then, the bishop called to the crowd.

"And we have our first box to bid on," he said.

Jeremiah Beiler picked up a rather plain cardboard box decorated with a single red-and-yellow parrot tulip. As he lifted the box for everyone to inspect, he sniffed the lid.

"Hmm, something smells good inside. Some meat loaf and apple pie, would be my guess," he said.

Dawdi Zeke bumped Dale Yoder with his shoulder and waggled his bushy gray eyebrows at the boy. "You should bid on it, *sohn*. It might belong to that pretty little Lenore you're so keen on."

The crowd laughed and Dale's face flamed bright red. Everyone knew he was crazy about Lenore Schwartz. In fact, they all expected the two to marry once they were old enough.

"That's not mine. I made ham sandwiches, macaroni salad and doughnuts. Mine's the one on the end with the three red tulips," Lenore said.

The group laughed harder. No doubt Lenore was petrified Dale might bid on the wrong box. Or worse yet, someone else might bid on her box and she'd have to eat supper with them.

"Who'll give me five dollars for this box? It smells real nice," Bishop Yoder called.

One of the fathers raised his hand.

Bishop Yoder pointed at the man and the bidding began. "I've got five dollars, who'll give me ten?"

Another hand went up. The bishop got into the groove of the auction, his voice firing off in rapid succession. And just like that, Becca realized this event had been a smart idea. Within two minutes, the first box had sold for thirty-five dollars.

Will Lapp won the box. As Minister Beiler took his money and held the box out to him, little twelve-year-old Emily Hostetler stepped forward to claim ownership. Since she was so young, Will's wife, Ruth, joined them. And once Ruth's box was sold to old *Dawdi* Zeke, the group made it a foursome so there would be no perceived impropriety as they ate together.

The bidding continued and Becca soon realized they would indeed have enough funds to purchase the teeter-totter. She hoped they would make enough to also buy some new baseball equipment and bouncy balls for the playground. If they did really well, they might even be able to install a couple of swings. She couldn't be happier and counted the day as a great success.

"*Ach*, this box smells like fried chicken," Jeremiah called, sniffing the rim of the lid with relish.

Realizing the box belonged to her, Becca's face heated up in spite of her desire to remain incognito.

"Who'll give me ten dollars for this box?" Bishop Yoder called.

Ben Yoder, the bishop's shy nephew from Iowa, held up his hand. With a rather quiet, retiring nature, Ben was large for an Amish man. He stood at six feet four inches tall and weighed about a hundred and ninety pounds, all of it lean muscle. His shoulders were wide as a broom handle and his hands were huge and strong. A lot of rumors followed his name. Bishop Yoder called him Gentle Ben but Becca had heard he'd had trouble with fighting in Iowa and had even killed a man in self-defense, which was why he'd relocated here to Colorado. It seemed that many of their people were trying to escape a shadowed past. With so many members of their *Gmay* around, she was willing to eat supper with him but had no romantic inclinations toward him whatsoever.

"I've got ten dollars. Who will give me twenty?" Bishop Yoder shouted at the crowd.

Becca saw Jesse King lift his hand in the air. His expression was stoic, his eyes unblinking as he gazed steadily at the bishop. As if in slow motion, Becca watched as the bidding bounced back and forth between Jesse and Ben until, finally, Jesse won her box for a price even she could never have anticipated. Did he know that it was her box? Had Abby told him? Or was it just a coincidence? Becca had no idea.

She stared, her mouth dropping open in absolute surprise. On the one hand, she was delighted that Jesse would pay so much for her box. But on the other hand, she was mortified at the outlandish amount of money.

"Sold! To Jesse King for seventy-five dollars," the bishop cried.

A low murmur of awe swept over the crowd. Everyone recognized what a high price he'd paid. A subtle flicker of a smile curved Jesse's lips upward as he stepped over to receive his box. Becca didn't move. She didn't breathe. Her feet felt as if they'd been nailed to the ground. Finally, Aunt Naomi gave her a slight push forward and she took several steps.

A titter of chatter filled the air as everyone discussed this turn of events. No doubt the entire *Gmay* would be thinking she and Jesse were an item. That they were sweet on each other. And they weren't. But people wouldn't know that. Jesse wasn't interested in her. Or anyone else, for that matter. That thought brought an aching pain to Becca's heart. And that's the moment she realized she loved him. Heaven help her, she truly did. Somehow, during the past months she'd been working with Sam and Jesse, she'd fallen in love with both of them. Not just the love from serving other people, but a lasting feeling that made her want to be with them always. To take care of them and be a part of their life forever. Jesse might not think twice about her. Her box was filled with food that was quickly consumed and enjoyed but then forgotten. But for Becca, she couldn't think about anything but him.

"I guess I bought your supper." Jesse spoke low when Jeremiah handed him the box.

She looked at him, feeling trembly and confused by her new realization. She stared up into his eyes, not knowing what to say. She only knew she loved this man and his little boy. Every time she was near him, she felt twitter-pated. And when they were parted, she could think of nothing but seeing him again. Her heart went out to him and Sam, for the pain and sadness they'd been through. She longed to make them happy. To see them both smile and hear their laughter again and again. Over time, the sting of Vernon's betrayal had eased and she realized she'd never really loved him. Not like what she felt for Jesse. Not the romantic love a woman should have for a man she wanted to marry. Now that she'd had some time away from Vernon to think clearly, she realized her love for her ex-fiancé was simply a habit built up over years of being good friends. But what she felt for Jesse was so much more. An overflowing desire to be with him and make good things happen in his life.

Yes, she loved Jesse King. And knowing he could never love her in return hurt most of all.

"*Ja*, you bought my supper. I hope it was worth it." She spoke the words in a whisper, forcing herself to look away. Because she knew, if she didn't, she would start to cry and she couldn't stand to have Jesse and the rest of the *Gmay* witness such shame.

Opening his wallet, Jesse counted out the bills and paid Darrin Albrecht, their deacon, the required amount. Becca stared as their work-roughened hands made the exchange. She still couldn't believe Jesse had paid such an exorbitant price for her simple supper.

Picking up a small blanket she'd brought, she followed Jesse as he led her off to a grassy mound beside the creek bed. They were just beyond the crowd and, though they had some privacy, anyone could see them if they stepped over the incline.

Sam didn't follow, but hung around the barbecue, waiting for a hamburger or hot dog, courtesy of the school board. He raced around the yard with little Andy Yoder, laughing and joyful as can be.

"He seems happy today," Becca said, jutting her chin toward the little boys.

"*Ja*, he's been much happier since you came into his life," Jesse said.

Becca shivered at his words, wishing she could remain in Sam's life. Wishing she could remain with Jesse too.

Holding her silence, she spread the blanket across

the spring nubs of grass that were just beginning to grow along the creek bed and watched as Jesse sat down with her box.

"Did you know this was mine?" she asked, her mind whirling with wonder. If he did know, why did he buy hers and not someone else's?

"*Ja*, I must confess, I overheard your aunt Naomi talking to Abby about it."

So. Abby hadn't told on her but he had known and, if the high price was any indication, he'd made sure he bought it anyway.

She knelt on the blanket and lifted the lid of the box before setting the golden fried chicken, potato salad, fresh-baked rolls and peach cobbler within arm's reach. She watched as he picked up a drumstick and bit into the crisp, juicy meat.

"You paid way too much for this meal," she said.

He chewed thoughtfully before taking another bite and she watched him in silence.

"It was for a *gut* cause," he finally said.

She wasn't so sure. Seventy-five dollars was a huge amount of money to pay for a chicken supper. But there were so many questions she longed to ask him. So much she wanted to say. He had just paid a small fortune for her supper. Maybe he was interested in her after all.

"It seems that Sam isn't suffering any aftereffects from the fire safety class," Becca said.

Jesse looked at her, then studied his son. Sam stood near the creek bed with Andy and was holding a huge hamburger with both hands as he took a bite. The burger looked way too big for such a small boy and Jesse smiled at his eager efforts.

"*Ne*, he seems to have forgotten all about it, though I know that isn't true," Jesse said.

"When you picked up the book of matches and lit one, it was like a fire started inside him too. If I had known he might react that way, I would have excused him from the class," she said.

Jesse remembered how it impacted him as well. Until that day at school when he'd taught fire safety to the children, he'd believed he could never fight fire again. Now that it was over with, he realized he could. He just needed to be careful and vigilant at all times so another tragedy didn't strike his *familye* ever again.

He nodded, taking a spoonful of potato salad. The tang of the dressing was delicious and he wasn't surprised. Becca was an exceptional cook but he wasn't concentrating on his meal just now. "It probably did. You see, I caught Sam and Susanna, his younger sister, playing with matches. I really got after them and explained the dangers but it didn't seem to sink in. My house burned down a week later." The memory caused his voice to catch and he had to cough, blinking back the burn of tears.

She glanced down at the purplish scars covering his hands and forearms. They were ugly and a constant reminder of his failure. He flinched when she reached out and traced one scar with her fingertips.

"From what I can see, you did try to save them. You should wear these scars like a badge of courage," she said.

He blinked, his throat suddenly clogged with emotion. He coughed and took a quick sip of apple juice from a flask she had set nearby. He finally spoke softly, feeling as if his voice wasn't his own. "I… I tried but I was too late. I found Sam in the barn. All he would say was that it was his fault. I figured he must have been playing with matches again."

Becca cringed and he wished he'd never told her. This wasn't light conversation. They should be laughing and talking about simple, inconsequential things like the weather, the school and things going on in their community. Not the death of his *familye*.

She released a little sound of sympathy. "I'm so sorry, Jesse. But surely you understand you must forgive yourself and Sam for what happened. If you'll let it, the Atonement of Jesus Christ can wash away any pain you might feel over losing your *familye*. And Sam needs you now more than ever."

He agreed but forgiveness was easier said than done. In his heart, he knew what she said was true. And finally, because of her, he'd had the courage to pray and seek strength from the Lord. It was time, wasn't it? But forgive himself? He wasn't sure he could ever do that.

"It's taken me a long time to admit it, but it wasn't Sam's fault. He was only five at the time. Barely old enough to understand what he was doing," he said with a heavy sigh.

"Have you told Sam that?" she asked.

Jesse went very still, his mind frozen in thought. No, he hadn't. But maybe he should.

"Perhaps that's why Sam doesn't speak," she said.

"Because he blames himself, just like you do. You know, your *vadder* was too stern with you but you don't have to be that way with Sam. You're not your *vadder*. You are your own man. A *gut* man of *Gott*."

He didn't know what to say. No, he wasn't his father. He could be different. He could be a better man. Couldn't he? But he sure didn't feel like a good man. Not in a very long time.

He looked at her, thinking he shouldn't have told her so many personal things. He'd laid his heart bare. As he gazed into her eyes, he felt locked there. Mesmerized by the deep blue of her beautiful eyes. And before he knew what was happening, he leaned close and kissed her. A soft, gentle caress that made him feel alive and happy for a brief moment in time.

She breathed his name on a sigh and lifted her hand to place it against his chest. Her palm felt warm and he wished they could stay like that forever. But the contact was like lightning and he jerked away.

"I... I'm sorry. I shouldn't have taken liberties. I apologize for my actions," he said.

She looked away, her cheeks filled with heightened color. "I'm sorry too. I know how much you love your wife."

He came to his feet, glancing around to discover if anyone had seen his shameful actions. Thankfully, no one seemed to have noticed…except for Sam. The boy stood beside the creek a short distance away, his eyes wide with confusion. And suddenly, Jesse felt as if he and his son were the only two people there. For several long, pounding moments, Sam just looked at his father. And then, the child turned and ran to the back of the schoolhouse where Jesse couldn't see him anymore.

Oh, no! What had Jesse done? He felt the familiar weight of guilt settling inside his chest again. No doubt, he had upset Sam with his actions. After all, Becca wasn't the boy's mother. And he couldn't believe he'd been so disloyal to Alice. Why had he kissed Becca? She wasn't the love of his life. She wasn't his wife and never could be.

"I... I think I had better go and check on Sam. *Danke* for the delicious supper," he said, turning away.

Becca stopped him, coming to her feet as she handed him a pie tin of peach cobbler. He caught the sweet aroma of sugar and cinnamon. The oatmeal crust looked golden, bubbly and cooked to perfection.

"Here, take this with you. You paid a steep price and should have all of your meal. I hope you and Sam enjoy it," she said.

He took the plate, holding it with both hands. Feeling numb and empty inside. And as he walked away, he knew he had another huge problem on his hands. One that he'd never thought would trouble him again for as long as he lived.

He was in love with Becca Graber. In spite of fighting his own emotions, he knew it with every fiber of his being. She was like a breath of fresh air after being locked inside a cave for a year. And yet, he couldn't act on it. Never again. Because his devotion to Sam and Alice must come first. He couldn't betray his sweet wife's memory by loving someone else. Nor could he disappoint Sam, who was still missing his mother. Not after all that had happened. No doubt the boy saw this as a betrayal to his mother. Jesse felt the same way and was disgusted by his actions. He could never let down his guard with Becca again. No sir, not ever.

Chapter Thirteen

The following week, Becca returned to Jesse's house to tutor Sam as usual. Except this time, she felt more cautious than ever. Jesse had kissed her, or she had kissed him, she wasn't sure which. She was certain of one thing. It had been a mistake. Jesse still loved his wife and Becca had chosen a career in teaching. She wasn't about to be sidetracked. Vernon had played with her emotions often enough, holding her hand and declaring his love just days before he'd ended their engagement. It had all been a lie. He'd been leading her on for over a year because he didn't know how to break things off with her. And all that time, she'd allowed herself to believe he really cared. But after she'd learned the truth, she'd promised herself she'd never fall into that kind of trap again. She couldn't trust men to be honest with her. It was that simple.

On the ride to Jesse's farm, Sam didn't speak. He frowned and wouldn't meet her gaze. After witnessing his father kissing her and then running away, she feared he might not like her anymore. He'd been overly withdrawn at school all day and she thought he must be angry with her. And she couldn't blame him. No doubt he thought she was trying to usurp his mother's place. Because he didn't talk a lot, she dreaded asking him about it. Since she'd be leaving town soon, it didn't really matter but she'd rather part as friends.

"Are you ready for your lessons?" she asked as they climbed out of her buggy and she carried her book bag up the steps. She was trying to act normal.

He nodded and opened the door so she could come inside. The kitchen looked orderly, no dirty dishes in the sink. There was nothing cooking on the stove for supper but it was early yet.

"I wonder where your *vadder* is." She set her bag on a chair and removed her black traveling bonnet.

Sam pointed toward the barn. No doubt Jesse was still working. It was just as well. Maybe she could finish Sam's lessons and depart before Jesse came inside. Then they wouldn't have to speak. They could forget the kiss ever happened and go on with their lives as usual.

"*Ach*, let's get started then," she urged.

As she pulled out a chair, she eyed the boy surreptitiously. He didn't look at her as he placed his reading book, note paper and pencil on the table and promptly sat down to wait. Hmm. Was he avoiding her? Maybe he was more upset than she thought.

They went through their normal routine with one exception. Sam didn't speak to her in his usual soft whisper. Not even once. And when they finished their studies, she slid her own books into her bag and looked at Sam, thinking what she could say to ease the tension between them.

"Sam, I hope you're not upset with me. I'm so sorry if I've done anything to hurt your feelings. I know how much you love your *mudder*. And no one will ever take her place. She'll always be your *mudder*. I just want to be your friend," she said.

He peered at her with his big, round eyes before finally nodding. And though he didn't speak, she knew his body language well enough to believe he'd accepted her apology. But oh! How desperately she wished he would smile again. He looked so gloomy that she wanted to cheer him up.

"I'll tell you what. Before I leave, why don't we play a game of hide-and-seek just for fun? Would you like that?" She hoped he agreed. She'd seen him playing with Andy at recess and thought he enjoyed the game. In dealing with children, she'd learned that if she could make them smile, they seemed to trust her more willingly. And that was her goal now. To win back his trust.

"All right, do you want to count and be the seeker, or would you rather hide first?" she asked.

He covered his eyes with his hands to indicate he'd like to be the seeker.

"*Ach*, the kitchen table can be our home base. Close your eyes and count to one hundred. And no peeking." She laughed as he ducked his head over his arms. Because he didn't make any sound, she wasn't sure if he was counting but realized she had better get moving.

Hopping up from the table, she hurried into the living room and looked for a place to hide. She ended up crouching behind the sofa. Within moments, she heard him step over the threshold from the kitchen. She waited, holding her breath. When she thought he'd moved away from her, she bolted toward the kitchen…and ran smack-dab into Jesse's chest.

"Oh!" she cried, looking up into his startled gaze.

"What are you doing?" he asked, seeming just as surprised as she was.

Beyond him, she saw Sam standing in the kitchen doorway. His eyes were round with confusion.

"I… I was playing hide-and-seek with Sam. I thought you were him coming to catch me," Becca said.

She gazed at the damp hair that curled around Jesse's face. He'd removed his straw hat and held it in one hand. As was his normal routine, he must have washed out in the barn. To catch herself, she'd lifted a hand to clasp his upper arm and felt his solid bicep beneath her palm. She caught his scent, a mixture of clean hay and horses. And then, thinking how odd the situation must seem to Jesse, she burst out laughing.

"Ahem!"

In unison, they both turned and got another shock. Bishop Yoder stood just inside the front door. His bushy eyebrows were drawn together in a deep frown and his piercing gaze was pinned on them. Recovering her senses, Becca released Jesse's arm and stepped back fast, putting some distance between them. What must the bishop think, seeing them like this? She could only imagine. She blinked and felt her face flood with heat.

"I'm sorry to interrupt but I knocked twice. You didn't seem to hear me, so I came inside," the bishop said.

Jesse tossed his hat on the coffee table. Lifting a hand, he stepped over to greet the bishop.

"*Ja, komm* in. *Komm* in!" Jesse welcomed him with a smile but Becca could tell from his tensed shoulders that he was just as nervous as she was.

The bishop shut the front door and removed his black felt hat. He wore his frock coat, which indicated he was there on official church business. Becca couldn't help wondering what that was and she hoped it wasn't serious.

Looking straight at her, the bishop's eyes were unblinking as he asked her a pointed question. "Miss Graber, what are you doing here?"

She almost groaned out loud. Instead, she swallowed hard, knowing how this must look. Why did Bishop Yoder have to walk in on them just now? Why couldn't he have come earlier, when she was sitting primly at the kitchen table with Sam as they went over his studies? Why did he have to see her laughing and touching Jesse in a most improper way?

She opened her mouth to explain but no sound came out. She felt muddled and tongue-tied.

Jesse cleared his throat. "Miss Graber tutors Sam several afternoons each week, to help with his speaking problem."

Bishop Yoder's forehead crinkled as he thought this over. "I knew Miss Graber was tutoring Sam but

I had no idea she was coming here to your home to do it. It isn't proper for a young, single woman to be coming here like this."

Oh, dear. The bishop didn't need to enlarge on the issue. Becca knew what he was thinking. She was the schoolteacher and must set a good example for the Amish children under her tutelage. When she'd started tutoring Sam, she hadn't thought that it might look bad for her to come here several afternoons each week. Even her *familye* members knew she was here and no one had ever suggested that it wasn't right. And everything would have probably been fine, except that the bishop had seen her behaving in a silly, unladylike manner. Not like the proper schoolteacher she was trying to portray.

"Becca has been nothing but proper while she's been here in my house. And Sam's schoolwork has greatly improved because of her efforts. She has been very generous with her time," Jesse said.

Oh, bless him for defending her. Becca was beyond grateful but feared it wouldn't help. Not this time. The bishop was a kind, nonjudgmental man but he was still the leader of their *Gmay*. The situation was bad enough that it could cause her to lose her teaching recommendation and she'd never be given another assignment again.

"I'm sorry, Bishop Yoder. I meant no harm. You see, I was playing hide-and-seek with Sam. I thought Jesse was him and I bumped into him and…" Her words trailed off. She was babbling and making no sense. What good would it do to try and explain? She knew how it looked and it wasn't good.

The silence was deafening as the bishop studied both her and Jesse for several long, torturous moments. The church elder's steely gray eyes were unblinking as he considered her. She waited with bated breath, not daring to say another word that might make matters worse.

"I trust this will never happen again," the bishop finally said.

Becca shook her head and quickly reassured him. "*Ne*, I won't come here alone again. In fact, Sam and I were finished for the night. School is almost out and... I was just leaving."

"*Gut*. Your lessons here are finished. You can tutor Sam at school from now on."

Though the bishop spoke gently, his words were an order, not a request.

She nodded and he watched as she hurried to the kitchen, gathered up her things and fled out the back door.

Jesse watched her go, his expression pensive. She knew how serious the situation was. It was no laughing matter. If the bishop thought there was any impropriety, both she and Jesse could find themselves shunned for any number of weeks deemed appropriate by the church elders.

As she hopped into her buggy and directed the horse down the lane, she glanced over and saw Sam standing on the back porch watching her. She lifted a hand to wave at him but he didn't respond. And as she drove home, three things troubled her mind. First, she worried that Sam hadn't fully forgiven her for seeming to usurp his mother's place. And it was beyond mortifying to her that the child might think she was making a play for his father. Because she wasn't. Not at all.

Second, she feared her teaching recommendation might now be in jeopardy. And she needed that to secure another position in the fall.

And third, she hoped she hadn't just created a huge problem for Jesse. After all, she was a young, unmarried woman and innocent to the world. But Jesse was a father and a widower and the bishop might hold him to a higher standard. She didn't want him to get into trouble because of her. Because she loved them, all she wanted was for him and Sam to be happy.

Maybe it was a good thing the school year was almost over and she'd be leaving town. It was for the best. Wasn't it? So, why did the thought of never seeing Jesse and Sam again make her feel even worse?

Except for Church Sunday and a few glimpses on the playground when he was dropping Sam off and picking him up from school, Jesse didn't see Becca again for two weeks. Two long weeks of worrying about her. He'd wrestled with the idea of going over to her cousin's farm to speak with her but knew that could only make matters worse. And what would he say to her? That he loved her but couldn't offer her any promises because of his devotion to his dead wife? Not to mention Sam, who was still missing his mother and sisters too.

And now, the end-of-year program was here. It was the last day of school. After today, Jesse wouldn't see Becca again. He'd been told that she was leaving in a couple of days. Returning to her *familye* in Ohio until she could find another teaching position.

Jesse parked his horse and buggy in the main schoolyard, then helped Sam hop down. Other parents were arriving with their kids and they greeted him. He waved, thinking how they had welcomed him and Sam into their community. The men had taken him with them to the livestock auctions and he now had four beautiful draft horses and another milk cow. They'd been kind to him and he felt almost relaxed around them now.

With his head down, Sam walked silently beside him as they entered the schoolhouse. While Sam went to sit at his desk, Jesse stood at the back of the room with the other parents. The bishop was there and gave him a friendly nod, not showing any sign that he was upset with him in the least. Becca stood beside her desk, rifling through some papers. Because he knew her well, the heightened color in her face told him she was slightly flustered. But to everyone else, she looked completely composed and in control.

She set the papers aside on her desk and stood up straight, her hands folded in front of her, a genuine smile on her face. "*Guder mariye*, scholars."

"*Guder mariye*," the children responded in unison.

Becca looked at the parents. Her gaze clashed then locked with his. In that brief moment of time, he saw what he thought was a painful longing in her eyes. But then it was gone and he thought he must have imagined it.

"*Guder mariye*, parents," she said.

As a group, the adults in the room responded in kind, each one looking delighted to be here. After all, this was a culmination of an entire year of hard work and they were happy to see their children's progress.

"We are pleased to *willkomm* you to our school and hope you enjoy the program your *kinder* have prepared for you." She took a step. "*Ach*, without any further delays, we will get started. If the scholars will please *komm* forward."

In a rehearsed fashion, the children rose from their desks and walked to the front of the room where they stood in a V-shape with the youngest children to the front and the older children in the back. Turning to face them, Becca lifted her hands and hummed a note. Then, she led the students in a German song that Jesse recognized quite well from his own childhood.

As the last note rang out, little Timmy Hostetler stepped forward and recited a poem from memory. His voice sounded soft and shy, with no inflection. And when he finished, he stepped back into place and gave an audible sigh of relief.

The parents in the room smiled. They understood how hard their children had practiced this program and they couldn't help being pleased.

The scholars sang several more songs in both English and German. Dale Yoder, the eldest boy in the school, served as the *vorsinger* and set the pitch for each song before the other children joined in.

All of the numbers were sung *a capella* and most were sung very slow, just like at church. The hymns were achingly beautiful, the scholars' faces sweet and earnest. And when they finished, there was no applause because they didn't believe in praise. But Jesse couldn't help reveling in Becca's success. She was a very good teacher and he couldn't help feeling proud of her accomplishment. She should feel good about what she'd done this year.

A few skits were shown by the scholars and most made the audience laugh. Tiny pieces of colored paper had been taped to the wooden floor so the children knew where to stand. But there were some moments of confusion when several of the students seemed to be standing in the wrong place. Becca glanced at the papers on the floor, frowned in bewilderment, then quickly redistributed the kids. It became obvious that the colored papers were not in the proper order.

One skit went quite badly when the scholars held up what appeared to be the wrong posters and their props had mysteriously disappeared. Becca quickly stepped in and sorted everything out, handing them new props to use, then stood back and tried not to look perplexed.

A snicker brought Jesse's attention to the side of the room and he saw Caleb Yoder whispering something to Enos Albrecht. Both boys chuckled, until Becca threw them a warning look. But Jesse couldn't help wondering if the two boys had hidden the props and changed the order of the posters on purpose, in an effort to cause mischief. Regardless, Becca was right on top of things, setting it all right. It spoke to her professionalism and how well she had planned and knew the entire program by heart. Jesse hoped Bishop Yoder and the other school board members had noticed all of this and took it into account when they wrote her recommendation.

When Sam stepped forward, Jesse's attention went on high alert. He'd been anticipating this day for months and eagerly waited with bated breath to hear his son speak out loud.

Sam stood at the front, showed a slightly insecure smile and took a deep breath. He glanced first at Becca, then looked directly at his father…and promptly burst into tears.

Before Becca could step forward to comfort the boy, he raced toward the front door. Pushing his way past the walls of bodies, he burrowed through them and fled.

Oh, no! Jesse's heart gave a giant leap of sympathy as he hurried after his son.

"Excuse me," he said when he bumped into Jakob Fisher and stepped on someone else's foot.

They parted the way and he didn't stop. He had to go after Sam. Just one thought pounded his brain. He must comfort his son and ensure the child was all right. At that moment, nothing else mattered in the world. Not his love for Becca, not anything. Because it was now obvious to Jesse that Sam was upset about his relationship with the pretty schoolteacher. No doubt Sam thought Jesse was trying to replace his mother in his life. And he wasn't. Jesse couldn't do that to Sam. Not after all that he had been through.

Yes, Jesse loved Becca so very much. But he couldn't be with her. Not now. Probably never. It was futile to even try. Sam must come first in Jesse's life. He was the boy's father and had a duty to love and protect his child above all else. And for that reason alone, their *familye* unit could never include Becca. Jesse had to accept that now. Because fighting it would mean that Sam would eventually walk out of his life too. And he couldn't afford to lose any more of his *familye* members. Not even for Becca.

Becca watched in horror as Sam ran out of the schoolhouse with his father chasing after him. She couldn't believe this was happening. First, the colored papers on the floor had been changed, then the props had disappeared and the posters had been rearranged in the wrong order. Since she had checked them right before the program started, it didn't make sense. Until she heard Caleb and Enos's muffled laughter. And she had no doubt the two boys had created more mischief. But out of the corner of her eye, she saw Bishop Yoder gazing steadily at his young son and knew she wouldn't have to do anything about the situation. It was the last day of school and she was finished teaching here. She had no doubt the bishop would take care of his son without her interference. But now, she had another problem. Sam had run from the room in tears and her heart almost broke in two.

Though her heart was racing, she calmly stepped over to Lenore Schwartz, the eldest girl in the school, and gently squeezed her arm as she made her request.

"Keep things going. I'll be right back," she whispered.

Lenore nodded stoically and Becca knew she could depend on her. After all, the girl had helped with most of the program and knew it by heart too.

Brushing past the gawking parents, Becca hurried outside to search for Sam and Jesse. She didn't know what she could do to help, but she had to try.

Out of her peripheral vision, she saw the flash of movement heading back toward the horse barn and followed quickly. One thought clogged her mind. The school board hadn't reprimanded her in any way or indicated they weren't pleased with her performance but she feared she wasn't going to get a good teacher recommendation now. Not after this. Coupled with the bishop finding her at Jesse's house when she was tutoring Sam, she figured the mistakes of the program might be the final nail in her coffin. And she dreaded returning to Ohio without any future employment options.

No! She mustn't think like that. She'd promised herself and the Lord that she would have faith. She was determined to put her trust in *Gott*.

"I… I'm sorry, *Daed*. It's all my fault."

She slowed, recognizing Sam's voice. The words were spoken quite loudly. Not in Sam's normally quiet, shy whisper. No, these were the words of a child filled with despair.

She glanced around the corner of the horse barn and saw Jesse sitting on a tree stump. His back was turned toward her as he pulled Sam onto his lap and held the boy close to his chest as he rocked him in his arms.

"Shh, don't be so upset. Everything's going to be all right now," Jesse said.

"I-I-I'm so sorry," Sam wailed over and over again.

Becca blinked in surprise. Sam had spoken to her several times in a pitiful whisper but he never spoke to his father. Not once since she'd known them. Now, it seemed as if the dam had finally shattered and the boy couldn't be quieted.

"It's all right. It's not your fault," Jesse soothed.

Becca realized they weren't talking about the school program at all. They were talking about the house fire. They were talking about guilt.

Pressing her spine against the rough timber of the barn wall, Becca clenched her eyes closed and didn't fight her own tears. She didn't want to interfere. Not now. She was too bold. Too outspoken for a proper Amish girl. That was one reason Vernon didn't want to marry her. As long as Jesse was being kind to Sam, she wanted to leave them alone. She'd said too much already. But she couldn't leave either. And so, she stayed where she was and listened to their mournful conversation.

"I… I didn't mean to kill *Mamm* and Mary and Susanna," Sam sniffled.

Jesse snorted. "You didn't kill them. You didn't."

"*Ja*, I did." The boy groaned and then he spoke in a frenzied rush, as if he were reliving what had happened all over again. "You were gone that night, fighting fire for someone else. I was the man of the house. It was my responsibility to make sure the chores were done and everyone was safe in bed. On my way out to the barn, I found Susanna playing with matches. I got after her and told her to put them away. She said she would and I went outside. I milked the cows all by myself and put the cans in the well house. But when I returned to the house, I saw smoke and flames through the kitchen window. I tried to run inside but it was too hot. I… I couldn't get to them. I heard *Mamm* upstairs screaming for Mary but she couldn't find her. Or Susanna either. And then, before I knew what was happening, the roof caved in. It was awful…"

Sam's words trailed off on a muffled sob. Becca pressed a hand to her mouth to stifle her own tears. In her mind's eye, she could imagine everything Sam had described. The horror of that night seemed all too real when she considered what Jesse and Sam had lost.

"*Ach*, listen to me, *sohn*." Jesse spoke gently, his voice firm. "The fire wasn't your fault. It wasn't. And losing your *mamm* and *schweschdere* wasn't your fault either. It was no one's fault. It was a terrible accident, that's all."

"But why did *Gott* let it happen?" Sam asked, his voice trembling.

"Because He gives us our free agency to act, even if it means there might be bad consequences. But that doesn't mean He doesn't love us. I want you to let it go now. I want you to be happy, not sad. It's time we both let it go," Jesse said.

"But… I miss Susanna and Mary," Sam sniffled, his words so pitiful that it broke Becca's heart.

"I know, *sohn*. I do too. So very much."

"And I miss *Mamm*. I wish she'd come back and we could be a *familye* again."

"I do too. More than anything else in the world. No one can ever replace her in our lives or in our hearts. We'll never love anyone the way we loved her," Jesse said.

Becca turned away, her heart wrenching. She couldn't listen to any more. She stumbled away, heading toward the school. She bit her bottom lip, ignoring the tears streaming down her cheeks. All of a sudden everything made perfect sense. No wonder Sam had run off when he'd seen Jesse kiss her. No wonder the boy seemed offish toward her that last day when she went over to his house to tutor him. And then, he had raced out of the school during the end-of-year program. Not only did he blame himself for his mother and sisters' deaths but he thought Becca was trying to take their place. She should have realized it early on but she'd been blinded by love.

Oh, how Sam must resent her. She was his teacher and had betrayed his trust. And Jesse too. He was loyal to his wife. He didn't want an opinionated schoolteacher like her to usurp his wife's place. Jesse didn't love her. His heart was too full of memories and devotion for his wife. He could never love Becca. Not in the same way. Not as a man should love the woman he was married to. And neither could Sam. Which meant they could never be together. Never be a true *familye*. It was foolish for her to think they could.

Realizing the awful truth, she stood outside the schoolhouse on the back porch and wiped the tears from her eyes. Jesse and Sam didn't need her anymore. If what she'd overheard was any indication, the two of them were on the road to healing and forgiving, both themselves and each other. It was a private moment between father and son and she was so happy for them. It appeared that they'd finally reconciled their anger and guilt. But it wouldn't make a difference for her.

She pushed several stray curls of hair back into her prayer *kapp* and smoothed her long skirts. This was the last day of school and she was still the teacher. She had a job to do and mustn't let her students down. She would go back inside, complete her assignments and present the certificates of achievement. And tomorrow, it would all be finished.

She didn't belong here anymore. Her teaching job was over with and it was time for her to return home to Ohio. And that was that.

Chapter Fourteen

Becca plucked a number of tacks out of the wall and set them aside before rolling up the various posters that had been hanging around the schoolroom. Wrapping a rubber band around each print to keep it from falling open, she stored them on a shelf in the back closet. She wanted to make sure Caroline Schwartz could find them in the fall when she came to set up the room for the new school year.

Becca picked up a bucket of sudsy water and carried it over to the windows. After wringing out a wash rag, she cleaned each windowsill and wiped down all the scholars' desks. She'd already swept and mopped the wooden floors, swept the ashes from the potbellied stove and cleaned the chalkboard until it gleamed silky black.

Laying her notebooks and pens inside a cardboard box, she checked her desk drawers one last time. She almost laughed when she found the rubber snake again. Someone had put it back in her drawer. Picking it up with two fingers, she threw it away, not wanting to leave it there to scare Caroline half to death when she returned at the end of August. Becca wanted to ensure she had all her things packed and ready to go. She was leaving early tomorrow morning, traveling by bus to Ohio. Anything she left behind would be lost to her.

Including Jesse and Sam.

Giving the expansive room one last look, she turned and froze. Jesse stood in the open doorway, wearing his black frock coat and vest, a white chambray shirt and his best pair of broadfall pants. He held his black felt hat in his hands, his clean hair combed and tidy.

"Hello," she said, startled by his presence. And all at once, a bubble of euphoria engulfed her, along with a feeling of bittersweet heartache. What was he doing here? She didn't think she'd ever see him again.

"Hallo," he returned, showing that slightly crooked smile of his. He moved further into the room, seeming tentative. As if he was a bit unsure of himself.

"You're dressed so nice today. Are you going somewhere special?" she asked, taking one step toward him.

"Ja." His answer sounded positive but not very committal.

She tilted her head in confusion. "Where are you going?"

His smile widened slightly, causing his dark eyes to sparkle. Oh, how she loved it when he smiled or laughed. It lit up her whole world.

"To see you," he said.

"*Ach*, did you need some more books for Sam? I'm afraid you'll have to go to the library and check them out yourself. You see, I'm leaving first thing in the morning and won't be able to do it any longer. I'm afraid that I..."

"Don't go."

He spoke low. So softly that she almost didn't catch his words. But she did hear. At least, she thought she did. Two little words that hung in the air between them, leaving her speechless.

"What...what did you say?" she finally asked, thinking her own wishes were causing her to hear things that weren't real.

He came to stand just before her. She stared up at him without blinking, feeling transfixed by his gaze.

"I said, don't go. Please stay," he reiterated.

Okay, so she wasn't hearing things. But what good would staying a few more days do them? It would only make the pain last longer.

She turned away, picking up a feather duster. To give herself something to do, she fluttered it across her already clean desktop. The movement gave her a badly needed distraction.

He gripped her upper arm gently, causing her to go very still. Slowly, he turned her to face him and she was forced to meet his eyes.

"I can't stay any longer, Jesse. I'm going home. I've got to find work. There's so much to be done. I've got to send out more applications and..." She rambled on, trying to convince herself that it was the right thing to do.

"I love you."

No, no! It couldn't be true. She couldn't believe him.

"Don't say things that aren't true," she snapped.

"But it is true. I mean it, Becca. I love you, so very much."

He tried to take her hand but she pulled away, refusing to listen. Vernon had said he loved her too and it had been a lie. Now, Jesse was doing the same thing. Telling her what she wanted to hear before he broke her heart again.

She kept on chattering away, feeling nervous with him standing so close. "It's been wonderful working here. I've loved teaching Sam and the other children but I have to go now."

"Becca! Listen to me. I love you! And I mean it. Please, don't turn away from me." His voice sounded a bit anxious, as if he were afraid.

She whirled on him, her feelings a riot of unease. Oh, how she longed to believe him. But what if he were lying to her?

"You don't mean it. Not really," she said.

"I do mean it. Every word. I'm not some silly boy, Becca. I know my own mind. I love you. Would you mind not returning to Ohio at all?" he asked.

She swallowed, thinking she'd misunderstood him again, yet knowing her hearing was fine. "I... I'm afraid that isn't possible now. I heard you and Sam yesterday, out back by the horse barn. I know you two have reconciled and Sam is speaking again. That's so wonderful. But my work is done here. I have to go."

He showed a slight frown, his gaze never leaving hers. "Hmm. You heard my conversation with Sam? All of it?"

She nodded, feeling her face heating up. She didn't like to confess that she had eavesdropped on them. "I'm so happy for you both. I know Sam loves and misses his *mudder* very much. So do you."

And she was happy for them. So very happy that they'd reconciled. That they could be a loving father and son once more. But she didn't believe that love included her.

"You didn't listen to our entire conversation, did you?" he asked, watching her quietly.

"*Ne*, I thought it was too personal. Once I realized you had everything in control, I returned to the schoolhouse." She wasn't about to tell him that she'd cried too. That even without him telling her he loved her, her heart was breaking once more.

"Then you didn't hear Sam tell me that he loves you too. Nor did you hear me explain to him that it's time for us to move on with our lives and be happy again. Or that Sam wishes you could be his *mudder* now and I want you to be my wife," he said.

She stared, too stunned to speak for several pounding moments.

"You…you told Sam that?"

He nodded. "I certainly did."

"And Sam told you he loves me?"

Another nod. "He did."

It was too much. Oh, how she wanted to believe him. But that would require her to take a leap of faith. To trust him.

"But Sam ran away when he saw you kissing me

at the box social. And then again during the school program." She felt shocked to the tips of her toes.

"*Ja*, he was still feeling guilty for the house fire. He didn't think he had a right to love you and be happy again. I told him that's not right. The fire wasn't his fault at all. I told him I love you too. I want us to be a *familye*." Jesse made the admission slowly, thoughtfully, as if he really meant it.

"I… I don't understand. Why would you say all those things?" She couldn't believe it. This was a joke. He was teasing her. Wasn't he?

"Because it's true. I love you, Becca. Please don't go. Don't break my heart. I want you to stay."

Don't break his heart? All this time, she'd been fearing he might hurt her, not the other way around. His plea made her want to love and keep him safe. To protect and cherish him the way she longed to be loved and treasured.

"But…but you love your wife. You don't love me. Not the way you loved your wife," she cried.

"My love for Alice was filled with a deep concern for her welfare, appreciation, respect and passion. That's exactly how I feel about you. I want to spend the rest of my life with you. I've fought my feelings for a long time but I can't fight them anymore. I love you, Becca. And if you'll have me, I'd like you to be my wife. I know it's what Alice would want for me too."

She gave a shuddering laugh of incredulity. This was happening so fast and she was having difficulty wrapping her mind around what he was saying. "Are you sure Sam feels this way too?"

"*Ja*, he loves you for being there for him. For helping us during a critical time in our lives. For never giving up on us."

She jerked when Jesse lifted his head and called to his son.

"Sam! Would you come in here, please?"

As if in a dream, Becca watched as Sam appeared in the doorway, holding his little straw hat in his hands. Like his father, he was wearing his Sunday best, his cheeks gleaming pink from a good scrubbing. It touched her deeply that the two of them had bathed and dressed in their finest clothes just to pay her a visit and…

They were proposing marriage to her! It finally sank in to her muddled brain. They were really here, standing in front of her, asking her to marry them. Jesse wasn't lying to her. He was speaking the truth.

"Teacher Becca, *danke* for everything you've done for me and *Daed*." The boy spoke in a soft voice but it carried clear across the room. Not a whisper. No, not at all.

Hearing Sam talk out loud like this was almost more than Becca could take in. She went to him and knelt down.

"Oh, Sam! You're speaking again. It's so *wundervoll*." Before she could think to stop herself, she pulled him into her arms for a tight hug. Her emotions almost overwhelmed her and she realized tears ran down her cheeks.

Finally, she released the boy and he stepped back, smiling wide. She stood and faced Jesse, her thoughts zipping around in her head like fireflies.

"I can't believe all of this is true," she said.

"Believe it, Becca. It's all true." Jesse took Sam's hand and the two gazed at her with such adoration, so much expectation and love, that Becca felt like she was living a dream.

"Last night, Sam and I talked it over in depth," Jesse said. "I realized that, if I didn't tell you how we felt, you wouldn't know and might leave us forever. Until you came into our lives, I didn't realize how much *Gott* loves and cares for me and Sam. You've helped me realize that, no matter how difficult life's trials might be, the Lord is always there for us. I know that because He brought us you."

Jesse reached inside his hat and withdrew a white envelope, which he handed to her. It had her name scrawled across the front and she recognized the bishop's handwriting. Becca took it with trembling fingers but didn't open it.

"In case you're wondering, it's a very glowing letter of recommendation from the school board. Last night, after you left the school, I explained to the bishop and other board members how much you've done for Sam and me. Bishop Yoder has heard reports from other parents as well and was in agreement that you are one of the most loving, caring teachers he has ever met. You always go the extra mile. Nothing is too difficult for you. Not when it comes to your scholars."

She blinked. "You did that for me? The board really wrote me a *gut* letter?"

He dipped his head in acknowledgement. "*Ja*, but I'm hoping you won't use it. I'm hoping you'll be willing to make another career change to be a wife and *mudder* instead. I know how much you love teaching and I want your happiness more than anything else. But I'd rather you remain here in Colorado with Sam and me. I want you to be my wife and Sam's new *mudder*."

"*Ja*, Becca. Please stay with us," Sam said, his voice loud and clear, as if it was gaining strength with every word he spoke.

"Oh, Jesse! Sam!" Tears of joy coursed freely down her cheeks. And just like that, the pain of Vernon's betrayal melted away into nothingness. Her heart was full of happiness, not pain. She knew deep inside that she could trust Jesse. That he truly loved and wanted her.

"I love you both so much," she said. "I never dared hope you could love me too. I thought… I thought I was unlovable and I didn't want to leave you but I didn't know what else to do."

Jesse stepped close and enfolded her in his arms. She clung to him, resting the palms of her hands against his solid chest. She fed off his strength, letting it fill her with such joy she could hardly hold it all. She didn't shy away when he kissed her deeply. In the background, she heard Sam's happy laughter.

Finally Jesse lifted his head and looked deep into her eyes. "You really love me too? Because I don't want to be hurt again either."

She heard the uncertainty in his voice and knew he'd feared her answer too. After all, it couldn't be easy to propose marriage when you don't know how the bride might feel about you.

As she gazed lovingly into his eyes, she reached up and cupped the side of his bearded face with her hand. "*Ja*, I love you, Jesse. So very much. You and Sam. I can hardly believe it's possible that he's overcome his silence almost overnight."

She glanced at the boy and saw his smiling face, his gleaming eyes. He looked so happy standing there, watching his father embrace her. He seemed so confident now. The complete opposite of the scared little boy she'd met all those months earlier when she'd first come here to teach school.

"Anything is possible with the Lord's help. You have healed our broken hearts. We have been so blessed," Jesse said.

"You are right. When we put our trust in *Gott*, anything is possible," Becca said, believing what she said. The Lord had truly worked wonders in their lives.

Jesse reached down and picked up Sam. Together, they shared a three-way hug, overjoyed by the day. They had each learned to put their faith in *Gott's* redeeming love and in each other. Becca felt an overwhelming trust in Jesse. She knew he truly loved her. That he was counting on her to love him in return. And together, she knew they would have a bright and happy future.

"You'll marry us, won't you, Becca?" Sam asked, resting his little hand on her shoulder. From the safety of his father's arms, he gazed down at her with expectation.

She wrapped her own arms around them both,

squeezing tightly, determined to never let go. "Of course, I'll marry you. Just try and stop me."

"That's *gut*, because I've already spoken to the bishop about it and asked permission from your cousin Jakob and *Dawdi* Zeke too," Jesse said.

Her mouth dropped open in shock. "You have? When did you do all that?"

"I spoke to the bishop last night but I went over to your place early this morning, after you had left the house."

"Really? You're very sneaky. I had no idea."

He nodded. "I asked them all to keep it secret until I could speak with you," he said.

Becca laughed, filled with more happiness than she ever thought possible. "I'm so glad you did. Now we have something wonderful to look forward to."

"*Ja*, we do. Years and years of happiness."

She couldn't agree more. This was her heart's desire. To remain here in Colorado with Jesse, as his wife. To become Sam's mother and hopefully have more children as time went on. And as they walked out of the schoolhouse and locked the front door, Becca realized she wanted nothing more.

* * * * *

Don't miss these other books in Leigh Bale's Colorado Amish Courtships miniseries:

Runaway Amish Bride
His Amish Choice
Her Amish Christmas Choice

Dear Reader,

Have you ever suffered a tragedy so great that you didn't think you could ever recover? In this story, the hero and his young son go through a loss so severe that the little boy can't even speak anymore. Their hearts are broken and they've lost their hope for a bright and joyous future. It takes time for them to learn how they can be happy again.

When we seek our Savior with a pure and contrite heart, the Atonement can wash away our angst and pains. It can cleanse our sins of commission as well as omission. It can heal our despair and mend our broken hearts. Through Jesus Christ's infinite mercy, the Atonement can comfort the lonely, heal the infirmities of our bodies and answer our cries in the darkest of night. As we seek Him with humility and contrition, the amazing gift of the Atonement can offer us a reprieve to salve all our weaknesses. And all we have to do is repent and seek Him.

I hope you enjoy reading this story and I invite you to visit my website at www.LeighBale.com to learn more about my books.

May you find peace in the Lord's words!
Leigh Bale

WE HOPE YOU ENJOYED
THIS BOOK FROM

LOVE INSPIRED
INSPIRATIONAL ROMANCE

Uplifting stories of faith, forgiveness and hope.

Fall in love with stories where faith helps
guide you through life's challenges, and discover
the promise of a new beginning.

6 NEW BOOKS AVAILABLE EVERY MONTH!

AN AMISH EASTER WISH
Green Mountain Blessings • by Jo Ann Brown

Overseeing kitchen volunteers while the community rebuilds after a flood, Abby Kauffman doesn't expect to get in between *Englischer* David Riehl and the orphaned teenager he's raising. Now she's determined to bring them closer together...but could Abby be the missing ingredient to this makeshift family?

THE AMISH NURSE'S SUITOR
Amish of Serenity Ridge • by Carrie Lighte

Rachel Blank's dream of becoming a nurse took her into the *Englisch* world, but now her sick brother needs her help. She'll handle the administrative side of his business, but only temporarily—especially since she doesn't get along with his partner, Arden Esh. But will falling in love change her plans?

THE COWBOY'S SECRET
Wyoming Sweethearts • by Jill Kemerer

When Dylan Kingsley arrives in town to meet his niece, the baby's guardian, Gabby Stover, doesn't quite trust the man she assumes is a drifter. He can spend time with little Phoebe only if he follows Gabby's rules—starting with getting a job. But she never imagines he's secretly a millionaire...

HOPING FOR A FATHER
The Calhoun Cowboys • by Lois Richer

Returning home to help run the family ranch when his parents are injured, Drew Calhoun knows he'll have to work with his ex—but doesn't know that he's a father. Mandy Brown kept his daughter a secret, but now that the truth's out, is he ready to be a dad?

LEARNING TO TRUST
Golden Grove • by Ruth Logan Herne

While widower Tug Moyer isn't looking for a new wife, his eight-year-old daughter is convinced he needs one—and that her social media plea will bring his perfect match. The response is high, but nobody seems quite right...except her teacher, Christa Alero, who insists she isn't interested.

HILL COUNTRY REDEMPTION
Hill Country Cowboys • by Shannon Taylor Vannatter

Larae Collins is determined to build her childhood ranch into a rodeo, but she needs animals—and her ex-boyfriend who lives next door is the local provider. Larae's not sure Rance Shepherd plans to stick around...so telling him he has a daughter is out of the question. But can she really keep that secret?

SPECIAL EXCERPT FROM

❧

LOVE INSPIRED
INSPIRATIONAL ROMANCE

Temporarily in her Amish community to help with her sick brother's business, nurse Rachel Blank can't wait to get back to the Englisch *world…and far away from Arden Esh. Her brother's headstrong carpentry partner challenges her at every turn. But when a family crisis redefines their relationship, will Rachel realize the life she really wants is right here…with Arden?*

Read on for a sneak preview of
The Amish Nurse's Suitor *by Carrie Lighte,*
available April 2020 from Love Inspired.

The soup scalded Arden's tongue and gave him something to distract himself from the topsy-turvy way he was feeling. As he chugged down half a glass of milk, Rachel remarked how tired Ivan still seemed.

"*Jah*, he practically dozed off midsentence in his room."

"I'll have to wake him soon for his medication. And to check for a fever. They said to watch for that. A relapse of pneumonia can be even worse than the initial bout."

"You're going to need endurance, too."

"What?"

"You prayed I'd have endurance. You're going to need it, too," Arden explained. "There were a lot of nurses in the hospital, but here you're on your own."

"Don't you think I'm qualified to take care of him by myself?"

That wasn't what he'd meant at all. Arden was surprised by the plea for reassurance in Rachel's question. Usually, she seemed so confident. "I can't think of anyone better qualified to take care of him. But he's got a long road to recovery ahead, and you're going to need help so you don't wear yourself out."

"I told Hadassah I'd *wilkom* her help, but I don't think I can count on her. Joyce and Albert won't return from Canada for a couple more weeks, according to Ivan."

"In addition to Grace, there are others in the community who will be *hallich* to help."

"I don't know about that. I'm worried they'll stay away because of my presence. Maybe Ivan would have been better off without me here. Maybe my coming here was a mistake."

"*Neh.* It wasn't a mistake." Upon seeing the fragile vulnerability in Rachel's eyes, Arden's heart ballooned with compassion. "Trust me, the community will *kumme* to help."

"In that case, I'd better keep dessert and tea on hand," Rachel said, smiling once again.

"Does that mean we can't have a slice of that pie over there?"

"Of course it doesn't. And since Ivan has no appetite, you and I might as well have large pieces."

Supping with Rachel after a hard day's work, encouraging her and discussing Ivan's care as if he were…not a child, but *like* a child, felt… Well, it felt like how Arden always imagined it would feel if he had a family of his own. Which was probably why, half an hour later as he directed his horse toward home, Arden's stomach was full, but he couldn't shake the aching emptiness he felt inside.

She is going back, so I'd better not get too accustomed to her company, as pleasant as it's turning out to be.

Don't miss
The Amish Nurse's Suitor *by Carrie Lighte,*
available April 2020 wherever
Love Inspired books and ebooks are sold.

LoveInspired.com

LIEXP0320